MW01277106

Anthra's Moon

The Adventures of
Ysabel the Summoner

Signe Kopps

Lily

Rainhorse Press
Portland, Oregon

Anthra's Moon

Second Edition

Copyright (c) 2013, 2017 Signe Kopps.

All rights reserved. This is a work of fiction. Any resemblance to real persons, living or dead, is purely coincidental. Except for the use of brief quotations in a book review, this book or any portion thereof may not be reproduced or used in any manner without the express written permission of the author.

For permissions and information, please apply to Signe Kopps at signekopps.com

Editing by Joanna Rose
Cover art by Amalia Chitulescu
Author photo by William Howell

Published by Rainhorse Press
631 NE Broadway # 542.
Portland, OR 97232

Paperback ISBN 978-0-9991290-0-5
Ebook ISBN 978-0-9991290-1-2

Acknowledgements

Many people helped bring Anthra's Moon to life. I wish to thank them for their generous support:

Joanna Rose for her excellent editing and telling me to be meaner to Ysabel.

Amalia Chitulescu for her exciting cover art for this new release.

Rhiannah Kopps, Nick Kopps, Douglas Rees, and Josie Rees for slogging through the first drafts. Great readers all!

Robin Kopps-Kopra for his eagle eye in spotting typos that slipped through countless reviews.

And for the many times I despaired of finishing my novel, thanks to Cmdr. Peter Quincy Taggart for his motto, "Never give up, never surrender."

To Bill,
for years of listening to stories
about a courageous girl, a friendly giant,
and the magnificent Anthra.

⤙ One ⤚

"Ysabel, leave those boys and come sit with me."
The red-haired girl turned from the two boys playing in the shallow end of the pond and looked up at the top of the grassy slope. Her sister Olenna sat in the shade of a willow tree, rocking Princess Lira in one arm and beckoning to Ysabel with the other.

Ysabel glanced back at the dark green water in the middle of the pond. She wanted to dive into the deeper water and swim through the weeds waving above the muddy bottom. She would escape the heat and her tedious life in the castle. She'd feel free again. She shook her head. Her sister would frown if she jumped into the pond as though she were a peasant girl cooling off after a hot day working in the fields.

"Ysabel," Olenna called again. Ysabel started up the slope and jumped when the boys kicked sprays of cold water, drenching her back.

"Hey," she cried. "I wasn't looking." She moved away from the pond and lifted the hem of her skirt to wipe her arms.

Prince Rowen, a sturdy lad of five years, pleaded with her to stay. "We won't splash you again," he promised.

"Stay, Ysabel," urged the smaller boy, Blane, Olenna's son and Prince Rowen's closest friend.

"I'll be back." She watched as Rowen grabbed Blane's hands and pulled him through the water, running faster and faster until he let go and they fell shrieking with laughter into the pond. They immediately sat up and furiously cuffed water at each other.

Ysabel walked up the slope, passing a nursery maid who sat in the grass out of range of the splashing water stringing blue and white flowers to make a bracelet. The boys' long day shirts were folded in her lap.

She reached the top of the hill and sat beside her sister in the dappled shade. "One more minute," she said, "and those boys will be up again and worrying that poor nursery maid."

Olenna laughed and laid the sleepy baby in her carry basket. Princess Lira yawned and opened her eyes as Olenna tucked a soft wool blanket under her chin. Bouquets of winter violets embroidered along the edge of blanket matched the blue-grey of the baby's eyes.

"Sleep well, Lira." Olenna draped her shawl over the top of the basket and pushed it deeper into the cool shade.

In the pond below, the boys were squatting with their heads close together. Olenna lifted her face to the sun. "This feels good." She wore a gown of pale blue wool and a bodice of dark blue wool laced with silver cording.

Ysabel smoothed her new wool skirt and linen blouse that Olenna had given it to her when she came to live at the castle. "You work in the embroiderer's room now," she said to Ysabel. "You must look as though you belong in the castle."

Pointed high-heeled shoes on Olenna's feet had replaced her old, blunt-toed boots. Ysabel wiggled her toes in her shoes and wondered if Olenna's feet hurt. Her own shoes were simple—an oblong piece of tanned cow leather stitched onto a flat sole and tied around her ankle with a thick leather string. The soles were worn so thin that Ysabel felt every pebble underfoot. She would have to stuff her shoes with straw to keep her feet warm in the winter. She hid her feet under her skirt; she didn't want Olenna to know she needed new shoes. Her sister would order tight new boots like hers and toss Ysabel's comfortable old shoes to the pigs.

That Olenna would throw out a still usable pair of shoes showed how much her sister had changed. Three months ago she had been a contented wife living in their village with her young husband, Robert, awaiting the birth of their second child. Robert died of summer fever a few days after the stillborn death of their baby girl. For days afterward, Olenna lay in the sleeping room of their cottage, weeping for her dead husband and baby while Ysabel and her mother cared for Blane. Only the message brought by a neighbor that Queen Ceradona sought a wet nurse for her newborn daughter had roused Olenna from her grief. She bathed, put on her best dress and walked to the castle with Blane. The queen approved of the clean and pretty young woman with her healthy son by her side, and Olenna had not returned to the village.

Two months later their mother died, leaving Ysabel alone in the cottage. Olenna attended the burial for the few hours the queen allowed her to leave the baby princess and brought an offer of employment for her sister in the castle.

"I'll work in the kennels?" Ysabel had asked, excited about caring for the king's silky-eared scent dogs.

Olenna laughed. "No, that's work for boys; you will learn embroidery."

Ysabel had silently groaned at the news. Sitting indoors all day sewing small, perfect stitches sounded boring, but she was young and unmarried and could not live alone in the village. She agreed to come with Olenna. They closed their cottage and Ysabel moved into the castle.

Ysabel opened her waistbag and pulled out a stuffed lamb fashioned from a scrap of white wool she had swept up from the sewing room floor. The wool was from the lining of a red silk cloak ordered by Queen Ceradona to wear at the upcoming harvest festival. Over the past three weeks, while Ysabel learned to sew with silk threads that tangled at the slightest tug, the lead embroiderers sat before panels of the vivid silk, their fingertips freshly sanded as they worked gold thread, rubies, emeralds, and seed pearls into an elaborate scene on the back of the cloak, depicting the queen and her ladies gathering roses in a blooming flower garden.

Ysabel shook the toy, making the legs dance in front of Olenna's eyes. "I hope Blane is not too old for a stuffed animal."

"He will love anything you make for him." Olenna tilted her head and looked at Ysabel. "You sound more cheerful. You were unhappy the last time we talked. You missed your friends in the village and you didn't like sitting inside all day, learning your stitchery."

Ysabel rubbed the tips of her fingers that were covered with pinpricks. She disliked being indoors while the weather was fine. She was happier outside, stealing eggs from the seabird nests or searching the woods near their village for nuts and mushrooms to add to the family pot. But Olenna had brought her to live in comfort and safety at the castle and she did not want to sound ungrateful.

"I made a friend of the other apprentice. Her name is Adele. She's fostering with Lady Clara to learn fine sewing before she is wed. We're embroidering oak leaves on an old piece of silk. It's hard work. Lady Clara says the back of our threadwork must look as good as the front and she makes us pick out every stitch that isn't perfect."

She sighed and blew out a breath. "I dream of oak leaves every night."

"You have a lot of needlework before you," Olenna said. "I was surprised Lady Clara allowed you this half-day with me. She was laying out silks in the queen's chambers yesterday when I brought Lira in after her morning airing. Ceradona wants new dresses in every color for her visit to her father and mother next year. While I was there, she summoned John Cauldgate to open her jewel casket and give Lady Clara brilliants enough to adorn the new clothing."

Embroidering with silk thread was hard enough. Ysabel thought she would go blind if she had to sew a casket full of sapphires and emeralds and rubies on the queen's new dresses.

"John Cauldgate, the king's steward comes to the sewing room at night when Adele and I are sweeping the floor," she said. "He brings a big black book and sits with Lady Clara while she tallies the jewels the embroiderers used that day and counts the bronze needles in her box to make sure they were all returned and none were lost. We have to sweep again under the tables and embroidery frames if any jewels or needles are missing."

Ysabel glanced at her sister. "Lady Clara told us that we will work hard over the winter, embroidering the queen's new dresses. She said the king and queen will be gone all of next summer."

Her sister nodded. "They leave after spring sowing. The queen has not returned to Wymerin for two years and she is eager for her father, King Griffin, and her mother to meet their new granddaughter and see how well Prince Rowen has grown. They will return in late summer in time for King Jeramin and his men to hunt the stag and long-toed bears."

Ysabel tossed the lamb into the air and caught it. "Will you and Blane go with them to Wymerin?"

"Yes, of course. Lira needs me for another year and Blane is Prince Rowen's close friend."

"I don't want you to leave. What if the ship is attacked by pirates?" Ysabel did not want to be left behind. Adele would leave soon to marry and Olenna would be away on a long journey. She would be stuck inside the castle without her sister or her friend.

"We will be well guarded," said Olenna. "The king will not risk the safety of his queen and children."

"But the ship could sink in a storm. I've watched the sea in winter. The waves are taller than the king's biggest ships."

Olenna laughed. "Dear girl, the storms will be over by the time we sail and we'll return before the sea turns rough again in winter. I will be home before you know it. Now, enough worrying about the future, tell me about Adele."

Ysabel stuffed the lamb into her waistbag. "Adele was sleeping in Lady Clara's room but asked to bed with me because we're friends. We explore the castle together. Yesterday we climbed to the top floor and saw the door to the tower room. Adele told me that the door is made of iron and is so heavy that it takes two men to push it closed. She said the room is for royal prisoners, but it hasn't been used since the old King Breykker died. There's a little window at the top of the door. We wanted to look inside, but the window was too high."

"What of the castle guards? Were they about? Be careful, Ysabel, some of the men think every female servant is theirs for the taking."

"Adele tells me which men to avoid." Ysabel pulled her thread scissors from her waistbag. The two narrow blades were looped at one end to make a handhold. The blades overlapped in the middle and were fastened together with a bronze screw. She squeezed the scissors closed until the blades formed a long sharp point; good for stabbing. "Adele said to use these on any man who tries to interfere with me."

"You should take a page boy with you, Ysabel. I don't like you wandering around the castle."

Ysabel hastened to reassure her sister. "We are heedful. We walk together when we take embroidery to the ladies for their approval and we do not venture past the guardroom. Sometimes we pass men in the hall who try to talk with Adele. They call her little raven because her hair is black, but she's taller than me so I don't know why they call her little. We pretend we don't hear them."

"Good, don't speak to them." Olenna squeezed Ysabel's hand. "I have lived in the castle for three months and you know more than me after three weeks. From now on, I'll ask you when I want something."

"Ask me for anything and I will get it for you." Ysabel held on to Olenna's hand and ran her fingers over the smooth flesh. Her sister's skin was soft, no longer the rough-skinned hand of a village girl.

"I am thankful for my new life," Olenna said. "I want for nothing and Blane is happy. He attends lessons with Prince Rowen's tutors and is learning to fight and use a sword. When Blane is eighteen, he'll become one of Rowen's companions. That will be a great honor for my son."

"But what about you?" she continued. "Are you content to live in the castle or do you still long for home." Olenna smiled. "Does a young man wait for you in our village?"

"No one has asked for me yet, other than old Kirby." The woodmonger had brought a bundle of firewood and a basket of dove eggs for her after their mother died. He looked around the cottage, said it was tidy and that Ysabel would make a good wife.

"That man has been through three wives already," Olenna said. "And each one younger than the last."

Ysabel placed her hand on her flat chest. "I don't think anyone else will ask for me. I still look like a boy." She was relieved that she didn't look like a woman yet, ready to marry and breed. She didn't want to care for children or a cottage; she wanted to sail over the Drandelon Sea. She closed her eyes, thinking of an outcropping in the cliffs high above the crevasses where the seabirds built their nests. There she would sit and look out over the sea, wondering what lay beyond the green waters.

"You take after our father," Olenna said. "He was a small man. You have his hair, too." She pushed a strand of Ysabel's thin red hair behind her ear. "Be patient, my dear. One day a boy will ask for you and you will follow him gladly."

"I don't want to marry and have babies, not for a long time." Ysabel threw a stone toward the pond. "Muck and mire, I wish I were a boy. I would sail away on a merchant ship tomorrow."

"You're almost of an age to marry, then you will not think of traveling across the sea. And don't curse, Ysabel, you sound like a tavern girl. I don't want to hear muck and mire or eye of pig from you."

"Will you marry again?" Ysabel asked, eager to avoid a lecture on the evils of cursing and the sorry lives of tavern girls.

Olenna looked at her sister, not fooled by her attempt to turn the conversation. "Perhaps one day. A guard named Philip greets me when I walk with Lira in the garden for her morning air." She shook her head. "But I cannot return the smiles of any man while Robert and baby Emma live in my dreams."

They were silent for a moment. Ysabel said, "Will we ever go back home to our village?"

"I'll leave Queen Ceradona's employ after Lira is weaned, unless she has another baby for me to nurse. Until then, our neighbors will watch over our cottage and send word if the roof leaks or if it breaks from the weight of the winter snows."

"I will go home when you leave," Ysabel said. "I would not live in the castle without you."

"You will have learned a good trade by then and may not want to go back to our village. If your needlework pleases the queen, you could live and work in comfort for many years."

"Until my back is bent and my eyes are too dim to thread a needle."

"Don't rush to the end, Ysabel. Enjoy living in the castle. Your life is easier now."

"I miss being outdoors."

"I know, but you're fourteen years old. You're not a child anymore, free to roam the woods. I allowed you that liberty at home because you brought back nuts and berries, but we eat well now; you don't need to forage for food. Learn your craft and you will always find gentle work. Your position is sought after. I begged the queen to allow you to apprentice to the embroiderers instead of working in the kitchen or the laundry."

"She must love you to grant your request."

"She gave me this ring last night." Olenna held out her hand, displaying a sparkling band of sapphires on her finger. "And this new shift." She pulled up the hem of her dress to show the cream-colored silk underneath. "She is happy with me because her child thrives. Lira was born early and was so small the midwives feared she would die."

Olenna gazed at the boys who were smearing mud over their skinny chests. "Ceradona is lonely. The king has been gone for five days on his latest hunting trip and she has only her women as companions. She is with them all day and tires of them at night. She comes to the nursery during Lira's last feeding and talks to me about her father's kingdom. She says King Griffin's castle is so big that all of the rooms have never been counted and her mother's gardens are filled with so many flowers that on a summer's eve, the slightest breeze perfumes every room.

"The queen wants the same here and more. She designed a walled garden for her roses with hearths built into the bricks that will heat the air in winter to hasten the blooms in spring. I have seen the drawings, it is a pretty plan."

"The embroiderers say Queen Ceradona is ambitious," Ysabel said. "They say she wants King Jeramin to rule a kingdom as great as her father's."

Olenna nodded. "I heard her tell the king that he must tour her father's silver mines when they visit Wymerin next year and bring back a metal man to look for silver in the mountains north of Liridian."

Mining for silver sounded more exciting than sitting in a room all day, poking a needle through a piece of cloth. Ysabel imagined wandering through long tunnels dug deep inside the mountain, carrying a flaming torch and looking for veins of pure silver shining in the darkness. Perhaps she could talk Olenna into taking her to Wymerin so she could see a silver mine. She would be useful on the journey. She didn't enjoy sewing, but Queen Ceradona would need someone to repair her clothing and she could embroider new dresses for Princess Lira during the long visit.

"A mine would give work to men who have little land of their own," Olenna said. "It's hard work, harder than working the fields. The miners dig tunnels through the mountains to find the silver ore. They hammer the ore from the stone and haul it to the surface in baskets. The work is dangerous, Ceradona said that one year an underground river broke through a weakened wall of rock and drowned all of the men digging next to it."

Eye of pig, working in the mines was too hard. Ysabel did not want to break rocks all day with a lot of sweaty men or drown in a flooded tunnel.

"Would men of Liridian leave the fields to work underground?" she asked.

"They would if their holdings are small or if their crops fail. Most men would break their backs in the mine instead of watching their families go hungry."

"I remember when I was little and we almost starved," Ysabel said. "It was so hot that summer that the wheat burned up in the fields. Every plant in our mum's garden turned brown and died and the hens quit laying."

"Then the rains came," Olenna said. "The fields turned to mud and the chickens drowned in their coops. You were five years old. Mum and I ate every other day to save food for you. It wasn't enough, you cried all day because you were hungry."

She put her hand on Ysabel's shoulder. "Our life in the castle is good, but we would be dismissed in a moment if we displease the queen. So hear me, Ysabel, act the gentle lady and keep a careful tongue. Do not repeat the words of Lady Clara or the embroiderers or even your friend Adele to anyone but me. I learned when first I came to the castle that every word I spoke reached the queen's ear, so I smile and listen and say nothing that is not in praise of Princess Lira or Prince Rowen."

She yawned and turned to look through the willows at a low rock where a kitchen girl named Madron was pulling bundles of food from a large basket. Behind the girl, fields of yellow wheat swayed in the warm breeze.

"Help the nursery maid bring the boys to their dinner," she said. "I want to nap while Lira sleeps."

"Take your ease. I'll save a napkin of food for you."

"You're a good girl." Olenna yawned again. "Wake me when it is time to return to the castle." She moved into the shade and pulled her shawl from the baby's basket. She wrapped the shawl around her shoulders and lay down in the grass beside the basket.

Ysabel walked down the hill toward the pond where the boys were floating on their backs in the water. She heard a bell ringing and turned to see Madron standing on the rock, waving a hand bell. Ysabel called the boys, "Come out now, your dinner is ready."

"We are not hungry." Prince Rowen stood up, knee deep in water and crossed his arms over his chest.

Ysabel could not help laughing at the naked little boy acting the man. She said, "Cook put cherry tarts in the baskets."

The boys whooped and splashed out of the pond. They raced up the hill and grabbed their shirts from the nursery maid's hands. They pulled the shirts over their heads, picked up their wooden swords from the grass and ran through the trees, yelling and slashing at the draping branches.

Lira woke, crying at the noise. Ysabel hurried to pick up the basket before Olenna was awakened from her sleep. She stood in the sunlight, swinging the basket and humming until the baby quieted and closed her eyes. The morning was almost over. She would have to return to the embroiderers' room and stitch another row of oak leaves. She gazed at the pond, wishing again that she could dive into the cool water and swim away from her work in the castle.

Behind her, the nursery maid screamed, a piercing sound in the drowsy heat. She screamed again. Ysabel tightened her grip on the baby's basket and ran toward the noise, past Olenna who slept under her shawl.

The maid lay on the ground, covering the boys with her body. A half-eaten cherry tart was thrown beside her in the dirt. Madron crouched next to the rock. She turned her head when Ysabel emerged from the trees.

"Watch out," she cried.

Ysabel heard a harsh whistling sound, like the winter winds hissing through ice-covered trees. A dark shadow passed over her head, covering her completely. She was hit hard from behind and yanked off her feet. Her head slammed into a mass of warm feathers. Huge black talons gripped her waist. Long black wings on either side slowly moved up and down. She felt something on her wrist. White lice as big as barley ran from the black claws and up her arm.

"Let go, let me go," she cried, hitting the claws with her fist. At the sound of her voice, a gigantic bird's head with red eyes and a curved yellow beak twisted on its feathered neck and looked down at her. Ysabel's breath stopped in her throat at the sight of the impossibly big head. She heard Lira crying over the sound of the rushing wind. The baby was red-faced;

her eyes squeezed shut. Ysabel held tighter to the baby's basket, afraid it would tip and the princess would slide out and plunge to the ground.

The bird flapped its wings again, skimming over the wheat field, rising higher with each circling pass. On the ground below, Madron stood with her hand over her mouth, staring at Ysabel. The boys were yelling and waving their swords at the giant bird. The nursery maid knelt on the ground with her hands over her ears while Olenna came running from the willows.

Ysabel looked down at the yellow wheat whirling under her dangling feet. They were not as high as the top of the willows. If she could make the bird let go, she could hold the basket against her chest and turn in the air so she would land on her back. The wheat would cushion her fall and she would protect the baby.

She pulled at the claws around her waist, trying to pry them open. The claws were like iron hooks clasped together. She worked her fingers into her waistbag, pulled out her scissors and stabbed the tough skin above the talons. The bird shook its massive head but did not open its claws. Ysabel took a firmer grip on the scissors and drove the blades into the bird's foot, again and again, holding tightly to the basket while the bird screeched with pain. A black feather as long as a spear detached from one of its wings and zigzagged down toward the wheat field turning under Ysabel's feet.

The bird soared higher. Ysabel twisted her scissors deeper into the bird's flesh. The claws around her waist jerked open.

As she slipped from the bird's grasp, one of its talons snagged the baby's basket and ripped it from her hand.

Ysabel dropped through the warm air. She crashed on her back in the wheat. The breath was knocked out of her and she could not even cry out as the enormous bird flew away, clutching the basket with the screaming baby in its sharp, black claws.

❧ Two ❧

Queen Ceradona paced back and forth in front of Olenna and Madron kneeling in front of her with their foreheads pressed against the timbered floor. Behind the bowed women, a gardener wearing a dirty smock stood next to a long table with his hand flat on a length of paper to keep it from rolling up and disturbing the queen.

Two of the king's guards and a page boy stood at the outer wall, scanning the sky through tall glassed windows. The guards wore tunics of the king's men, dark green wool with a black boar embroidered on the front. The page boy wore the sky blue color of the queen.

In the corridor outside the queen's chambers, Ysabel peeked around the legs of a stout guard, trying to catch a glimpse of her sister. Her head ached and it hurt to breathe.

Olenna had found her in the wheat field and helped her stand while Madron and the nursery maid ran ahead, taking

Rowen and Blane back to the castle. When Ysabel could breathe again, the sisters hurried after the two girls, the heavy wheat whipping their waist and legs as they ran through the fields.

"What was that huge bird?" Ysabel had cried. "Where did it come from?"

"I don't know. Hurry, Ysabel, I must tell the queen that her baby was taken."

"Let her blame me," Ysabel said. "It was my fault, I let go of the basket."

Olenna turned to her sister, holding her side as she caught her breath. "No," she gasped. "Lira was my charge. I am responsible for her. You can help me by taking Blane back to our village. I do not want the queen's eyes to fall upon him while I am in disgrace."

Madron and the nursery maid had disappeared by the time Ysabel and Olenna arrived at the gates. A guard met them and said the boys were in the nursery and Madron had gone to the queen to tell her a giant bird had seized baby Lira and flown away with her.

Olenna ran up the wide steps at the front of the castle. Ysabel and the guard followed her through tall wooden doors and into the great hall. A group of kitchen girls stood around a trestle table in the hall, interrupted in their task of setting up the midday meal for the men in the castle. The girls gathered into a tighter group, staring at Olenna, Ysabel, and the guard as they ran through the great hall and up the stairs to the queen's chambers.

Ysabel had stopped behind a guard standing in the doorway. Queen Ceradona was sitting on a padded bench with her hands covering her face. Lady Clara sat next to her with her arm around the queen's shoulders.

Ceradona lowered her hands when Olenna ran into the room and dropped to her knees on the floor next to Madron. The young queen's eyes were red from weeping. A veil studded with small white pearls was half pulled off her dark hair. She stood and began to pace before Olenna and Madron, biting her lips and wringing her hands over and over. The pearl veil slapped against her cheek. She pulled it off and flung it to the floor.

She stopped in front of Madron. "Kitchen girl," she said. Madron raised her head. "You told the guards you know of the monster that took my baby. Tell me where it lives, tell us how to rescue the princess."

Tears rolled down Madron's cheeks and she spoke in a voice so low that Ysabel and the guard leaned forward to hear her words. "I don't know how to find her, my Queen. All I know of the bird is from stories my old granddad told us. He said he saw a gigantic bird when he was a lad working on a merchant ship. The ship was looking for fresh water and anchored near the canyons above the Sefrit Sea. Granddad said a huge bird that was almost as big as the ship flew out of the canyons. The other sailors called it an Anthra and said it lived in the canyons."

She continued, warming to her tale. "Granddad saw the bird again later that day. It was flying into the canyons,

carrying a big fish in its claws. Some of the crew followed it
into the canyons but they couldn't find its nest. They left at
night, when the harvest moon was rising. They went back the
next morning and found pieces of broken eggshells, bigger
than goose eggs, lying on the canyon floor, but they never saw
the Anthra again." She stopped, out of breath.

The queen put her hand to her mouth and let it drop.
"Does this Anthra have eggs in her nest? Is that why she took
my baby?" Her voice shook. "The harvest moon rises in three
days, did she take my child to feed her chicks?"

"My granddad did not say that the Anthra ate human
babies," Madron said, and quickly bowed her head.

Ysabel heard whispering. Two court ladies had arrived and
were standing behind her in the passageway. Both women
wore gowns of fine-spun wool. Their bodices were
embroidered with colorful jeweled flowers in the fashion of
the queen. The taller of the two ladies was the mother of a
young boy. She smiled as she murmured into her friend's ear.
Her son will be Rowen's new friend instead of Blane, Ysabel
thought. It was her fault. She let go of the baby. She should be
kneeling before the queen, not Olenna.

Queen Ceradona twisted her hands as she looked around
the room. She spied the guards at the window. "You," she
said. "Have you heard of this bird called the Anthra?"

One of the guards shook his head. "No, my Queen. I first
saw the bird this morning from the watchtower when it flew
over the fields. I could not believe my eyes, it was bigger than
anything I have ever seen."

Next to him, a guard with a pointed grey beard cleared his throat. "I once met a traveler in a tavern who saw such a bird flying over the Ashlon Sea. He said it was so immense that it hid the face of the moon. His friends laughed and said he was rum drunk that night and they saw nothing. But if there is a bird that big, then it must live in the land of the giants."

"And what of my baby?" she cried. "Are your men searching the fields? Mayhap the bird dropped the basket."

"I have sent guards out to look for it," said the greybeard. "One of my men sent a runner back to say peasants working in a field saw the bird carrying a basket as it flew toward the forests to the south."

"Oh, where is the king?" she wailed. "Why isn't he here to save our baby?" Her hand shook as she pointed to the guard in the doorway. "Send a messenger to King Jeramin and tell him what has happened. Tell him he must hurry to rescue our child."

"One has been sent," said the greybeard. "The king is on a long hunt. He may not receive the message in time to ride to the canyons before the night of the harvest moon."

"Then send another," shouted the queen. "Command him to ride without stopping."

The greybeard motioned to a guard near the door. Ysabel moved out of the way as he ran past her and down the stairs.

Queen Ceradona took a few steps, wringing her hands and halted in front of Olenna. Her gold-toed slippers were inches from Olenna's head. Ysabel held her breath, afraid the queen would kick her sister.

"My baby was taken because of you, Olenna," said the queen. "You should have died to save her. I give you six days. Three days for the king to find our baby and three days more to bring her home alive and unharmed."

She took a deep breath and continued. "If my daughter is hurt in any way, then you will be banished from Liridian. You and your son will be put aboard a ship and taken to Wymerin and there you will end your miserable days as slaves in my father's silver mines."

She turned to the guards. "Take her to the tower room. Her son is in the nursery, lock him up with his mother."

The greybeard and a younger guard helped Olenna stand. She sagged in their hands, her face red from weeping. The two court ladies drifted down the passageway to their rooms when Olenna appeared in the doorway. Ysabel followed the guards and her sister up the winding stairway to the children's floor. They stopped at the first door, the royal nursery. The maid who had attended the boys at the pond stood in the doorway with her hand on Blane's shoulder. Prince Rowen stood behind Blane with his wooden sword in his hand. He raised and lowered it, as if he wanted to protect his friend but was unsure if he should challenge the guards.

"Give the boy to me," Ysabel pleaded.

"No, he goes with his mother." The younger guard picked up Blane, who began to cry as his weeping mother was led past him and up another, narrower flight of stairs.

The guard put a hand out to stop Ysabel. "Do not follow, miss, or you'll join your sister in the tower."

The nursery maid shut the door. Ysabel stood alone in the passageway. Blane's screams became fainter as he and his mother ascended the stairs to the top floor and the room with the iron door. She heard footsteps and looked over the stone balustrade to see Madron leaving the queen's chambers, heading down the stairs to the main floor.

Ysabel ran after the kitchen girl. She grabbed her by the shoulder when they reached the archway leading into the great hall. "Tell me, Madron," she said. "What happens now? Is there time enough for the king to rescue the baby?"

Madron shook off her hand. "No, it will take a day of hard riding for the messenger to reach King Jeramin and many days more for the king and his men to search for the nest in the canyons, or in the land of the giants, or wherever the bird lives. The princess may be dead by then."

She backed down the passageway toward the kitchen. "I am sorry for your sister. She was kind to me. She did not yell when I was late bringing her breakfast."

"Wait. Is there anyone who can tell me a faster way to the canyons?"

Madron stopped to think. "The men who know the land beyond the forests are hunting with the king, but you could ask Daniel, the old leathermaker. He escorted Queen Ceradona on her wedding journey to Liridian. He may know the way to the canyons above the Sefrit Sea."

❧ Three ❧

Snippets of black thread littered the ground under the leathermaker's bench. Daniel sat outside the kitchen door with a leather breastplate in his lap. A leather basket filled with straps and pieces of armor was at his feet. The old man was threading a bronze needle as he listened to the pastry cook standing in the doorway with her hand over her heart.

"The sight of that bird would have stopped the breath in me," she said. "The smith told me a villager found one of its feathers in a field. He said it was black as night and long as a man is tall."

Ysabel stood behind a lavender bush in the herb garden, rubbing a stem of the purple flowers between her fingers as she waited for the cook to finish talking and return to the kitchen. At the far end of the herber, bricks of pale clay for the queen's new rose garden were stacked against the castle wall. A basket filled with mint leaves had overturned on the path, spilling dark green leaves into the dirt.

Life in the castle had resumed while the queen wept for her lost child. Two stable boys hauled buckets of water from the outside well, passing the smith's shed where the big man stood under his awning, tying on his leather apron. In the fruit orchards along the back of the grounds, small boys and girls climbed through heavily laden branches, picking yellow apples that they slid into net bags tied around their waists. When the bags were full, they handed them down to women on the ground who placed the ripe apples into deep straw baskets. Occasionally, one of the women would step away from the trees to look up at the sky.

The pastry cook glanced into the kitchen and turned back to Daniel. "Poor, wee baby. The queen cannot stop crying. I had not heard of this child-stealing Anthra. When I was a girl, my old mum frightened us with stories about a giantess with fiery eyes. She said the woman would catch us for her stewpot if we stayed outside after dark. I tell you, Daniel, I ran home from the fields every night as fast as I could before the sun set."

Daniel nodded as he stitched a cut along the bottom of the breastplate. "My mother told us about the tall man with no feet who stuck his head into open windows at night and sucked the breath from sleeping children. One of my brothers died when the tall man stole his breath."

"I fear the queen will not see her baby again," said the cook. "She sent a message to the king but I heard he won't receive it in time to save the princess." She waved at a boy entering the castle gates with a wicker cage of red sparrows tied to his back. The little birds fluttered inside the cage as the boy walked across the courtyard toward the pastry cook.

"Mind where you put the sparrows," said the cook as she led him into the kitchen.

Ysabel dropped the sprig of lavender and moved forward, stopping when the sparrow boy bounded out of the kitchen to stand next to Daniel. He watched the old man sew the last few stitches on the breastplate.

"I want to serve in the king's guard when I am a man," said the boy.

Daniel smiled at the lad, picked through the basket at his feet and pulled out a worn looking knife sheath. He slid the sheath on a leather strap and tied the belt around the boy's waist.

"Put a stick in this and practice drawing it like a sword," he said. "Start training now and when you are old enough you'll be ready to challenge for a place in the guards."

The boy ran toward the gates waving an imaginary sword. Ysabel approached the old man. Daniel wore a soiled linen shirt under a wool tunic and neatly patched hosen. His belt pouch was made of finely tanned leather. A brown wool cloak and a felted hat were tossed beside him on the bench.

He glanced at her while he knotted and clipped the thread. "You are Olenna's sister."

"I am Ysabel, good sir. I have come to ask your help in finding the great bird that took Princess Lira. I heard tell that you traveled through the countryside six years ago when you accompanied Queen Ceradona on her wedding journey. They say you might know the way to the canyons at the edge of the Sefrit Sea where the bird nests."

She dropped next to him on the bench. The words rushed from her mouth. "Please help me. The queen has vowed to banish my sister and her little boy from Liridian and send them to work in her father's silver mines if her baby is not returned alive and well."

Daniel shook his head. "I cannot help you, miss. I was a member of the queen's escort but we sailed across the Drandelon Sea from her father's kingdom into King Jeramin's harbor. We did not travel over the Sefrit Sea. I've never seen the canyons."

He laid the breastplate in the basket and picked up a shin greave with two torn straps. "Why do you ask the way, child? As you said, there is not enough time for the king himself to find the nest, be it in the canyons or in the land of the giants."

"Someone has to rescue the baby and save my sister from the mines."

Daniel picked up his needle. "Where is your father? Ask him for help."

"My father is dead and I have no brothers." She gazed at Daniel. His grey hair and wrinkled forehead made him look old and he was a little fat from sitting on his bench all day, but he had guarded Queen Ceradona on her wedding journey and knew how to wield a sword.

"Will you help me?" she said. "You'd be aiding the queen that you swore to protect."

Daniel rubbed his leg above the knee. "I cannot go. I'm lame. It's an old injury but it keeps me on my bench."

Ysabel let out a breath, annoyed by his unwillingness to help her. "Then tell me the way to the canyons."

Daniel scratched his chin with the tip of the needle. "See those trees?" He pointed the needle at the tops of trees visible beyond the castle walls. "That's the Darkmaren Forest atop the Darkmaren Hill. I have heard that the way through the forest is a shorter journey to the far end of the land where the Sefrit Sea begins. Few enter the forest. The king hunted it bare of stag and boar long ago and his woodward alone is allowed to gather nuts for his larder and wood for his hearth fire."

"How long would it take me to walk through the Darkmaren Forest?"

"You? You're a child on foot, you cannot travel alone."

"How long?" she repeated.

"If you start now and walk fast you might reach the far edge of the forest by nightfall."

She tapped her finger against her lip, thinking. "Then I would see the canyons?"

"No, beyond the forest is the Empty Valley. It would take you another day or so to walk across the valley and you'd still be a far distance from the canyons." He shook his head. "Give up this quest, my girl. There is not time enough to rescue the baby."

If Princess Lira were not returned, Olenna and Blane would be sent to the mines to break ore until they dropped dead from the hard work. They would die because she had let the giant bird steal the baby. Ysabel looked up at the trees and narrowed her eyes. Olenna would have recognized the sign that her sister was going to ignore her warnings to stay out of the woods and leave the last of the acorns for the hungry boars. She glanced at Daniel. I don't need his help, Ysabel thought. I can find my way through the forest.

The smell of roasting meat wafted out of the kitchen. Across the yard, two guards closed the main gates behind a brown horse pulling a large cart. A baker with his arms dusted white with flour, walked beside his horse with his hand on the animal's heavy neck collar. Sticking over the side of the cart was a long bone spike. Ysabel recognized it as the tailbone of a spikeback, the biggest fish in the Drandelon Sea.

The baker halted his horse, waiting as the guards dropped a long pole into iron hooks, securing the entrance while the men of the castle were at their meal. One of the guards pushed a shorter pole through loops set into a narrower door, bolting the gate that allowed one man at a time to enter the castle grounds. Both guards approached the baker. They ran their fingers over the tip of the spike while they talked with him. The baker nodded and led his horse into a side yard.

Daniel dropped his needle into his belt pouch. He stood, groaning as he stretched his back. He patted Ysabel's shoulder. "Go back to your sewing. There is nothing you can do to save the child." He left her to join the guards walking toward the steps leading to the great hall and their midday meal.

Ysabel stood outside the kitchen door. She needed food and her cloak for her journey to the canyons. She entered the kitchen that was busy with cooks and their helpers rushing to get out the midday meal. Ropes of garlic and onions and bundles of freshly cut herbs hung on hooks along one of the walls. The cage of red sparrows sat on a counter next to a big clay pot and a basket of large brown eggs. The birds chirped along with the voices of the cooks, who stood at the chopping table in the middle of the room, talking above the din about the giant bird and the horrible fate of the baby princess.

Pots of stew boiled in the fireplace. The odor of burning fat filled the kitchen as the boy in charge of basting a goose turned from the roasting spit to listen to the cooks.

"Mind the goose," yelled a cook and the kitchen boy hastily turned the spit.

There was no time for Ysabel to grab a slice of meat from the cooks and their flashing knives. She walked to a counter near a door at the end of the room and picked up a stack of round loaves of bread, trenchers meant for the dining table. She shoved a piece of the day-old bread into her waistbag and followed a group of boys and girls bearing platters of meat and cheese through the dark passageway and up the few steps into the great hall. She tried to snag a piece of meat in the passageway, but the boy with the platter moved away from her and into the big room.

A large window of painted glass adorned the wall over the closed main doors. Ysabel remembered Adele saying that King Jeramin had commissioned the window as a gift for his new bride, Princess Ceradona. Squares of pale blue glass framed the central picture of the king sitting beside his queen on a flowered turf bench in a sunny glade. A wreath of gold leaves flared out around the couple like rays of light celebrating their union.

Sunlight shone through the window, lighting the trestle table where Daniel and a score of men waited for their meal. The men were drinking ale and looking at a large map painted on the wall behind them that showed the land and the surrounding seas.

Ysabel set the trenchers on the table. A boy with a meat platter bumped into her and stepped on her foot. The worn leather string binding her shoe broke. She moved out of the way and knelt to knot the string again around her ankle. She took her time, looking up at the map while she retied her shoe.

The kingdom of Liridian and the green Drandelon Sea occupied the eastern corner. A half circle that looked like a bite out of the coastline indicated the small harbor below the castle. Beyond the walled villages and fields of golden wheat stood the king's forests. The woods were painted with a scene of King Jeramin and his men on a hunt. A wide-antlered king stag stood at bay, its breast pierced with arrows. Smallbears swayed in branches high above the snapping teeth of the king's hounds while black boars with their ivory tusks curled over their backs, hid behind leafy green bushes.

At the top of the map far above the king's lands, a forest of white trees marked the White Woods, the snowbound lands of the north. A few stick-drawn villages were scattered at the base of a snow-covered mountain rising between the White Woods and the cold Northfast Sea.

Along the western edge, the blue Sefrit Sea washed against sand-colored canyons, home of the Anthras. Ysabel stood and edged closer to the table, looking closely at the canyons. She hoped to see a black spot, anything to show the location of the Anthra's nest, but saw only a maze of canyons.

A round lake, deeper blue than the sea, was painted on the land in front of the canyons. Closer to Liridian a dab of brown stood for the Empty Valley, a stony wasteland bare of water, wheat, and trees. It was the country to the south, the land of the giants that held the men's attention. One of the guards unsheathed his dagger and tapped the forest on the far side of Breykker's Torch, the highest mountain in a range that curved around the giants' lands. The mountain was named for the old king who had driven the giants out of Liridian. The peak of the Torch was scorched black from the fire the king's men lit behind the retreating giants to keep them from turning back and reclaiming their land.

In the forests beyond the Torch, enormous men dangled the king's green-coated guards over their open mouths while giant women threw torn off human arms and legs into large cooking pots. Cottages as big as King Jeramin's castle lined the shore of the warm waters of the Ashlon Sea.

"That bird came from the land of the giants." The guard traced the journey over the mountain with his knife. "It would take us days to cross the Torch and look for the child."

The guard from the main gate spoke. "A baker passed through the gate before we closed it. He had a bone from a spikeback in his cart. He was bringing it for the king to hang on the wall."

The men looked across the hall at the trophy wall facing them. The wall was crowded with the stuffed heads of boars, king stags, smallbears, and long-toed bears. Above the heads hung a wooden spear the size of a tree that the old king had taken from the fallen chieftain of the giants. Below the trophies, the long table that was reserved for King Jeramin's companions and their squires was pushed against the wall until the men returned from the hunt.

"Old King Breykker wore a crown inlaid with pieces of this bone and a knucklebone from a giant," he continued. "Our king favors gold over iron, but he would welcome a gift of this spike."

The second guard from the gate spoke. "The baker said he took the tailbone from two swineherders who saw a big black bird, tall as a tree, who was carrying a spikeback to the top of a cliff. They chased it away before it could eat the fish." He lowered his voice and looked around the table. "The bird is hungry. That's why it took the child."

The guard with the knife nodded. "There are too few of us and not enough time to find the princess. We cannot save her." He sat down with the other men, picked up his tankard and used his knife to spear a chunk of meat from the platter on the table.

Ysabel watched, dismayed as the rest of the men turned from the map to their food. They had given up so easily! She was shocked that the king's guards, all strong and able men, were more interested in eating their meal than trying to save Princess Lira.

She took a deep breath and let it out. She had hoped to find men in the castle willing to help her, but there was nobody, not the fat leathermaker or a well-armed guard. She was alone in her quest.

❧ Four ❧

Ysabel moved away from the table, dodging a few hands that grabbed at her as she headed toward the women's sleeping room. She would fetch her cloak from her bed chest and then go back through the kitchen to steal a bit of meat and a knife. Her scissors were not weapon enough if she had to fight off the giant bird and save the princess.

She passed a wooden dais in the center of the hall where two high-backed chairs for the king and queen were placed. The royal chairs were carved from dark red garnetwood. When the king was in the castle, he and the queen supped in the great hall with his men and their ladies, enjoying the evening's entertainment of jugglers spinning wine-filled cups on sword point while their runty, excitable dogs jumped through flaming hoops. Harpers summoned by the queen plucked their stringed instruments and sang of love. Their words and music were often lost under the noise of the king's men who shouted and pounded on the dining table, upsetting tankards of ale as they blustered and bragged about the latest hunt. The room would grow quiet when the deep-voiced old poets appeared to recite the history of Liridian. The people heard again of the day, forty years past, when young King Breykker stood on the deck of his storm-battered ship and first sighted the island emerging from the morning mist, and claiming the rich, forested land in the name of his beloved wife. King Jeramin yelled with his men at the telling of the war against the man-eating giants who dwelt in the forests around Liridian, of King Breykker's steel against their sharpened wooden staves, and finally, of the king's killing throw of his iron spear that pierced the throat of the leader of the big men, bringing him crashing to the ground and ending the giants' resistance. They raised their tankards to the wedding of King Jeramin to the beautiful Princess Ceradona of Wymerin. At the end of the tale, they cheered the birth of Prince Rowen, the future king.

Ysabel hurried past the dais, ducking behind a pillar when she saw a plump little woman and a tall, dark-haired girl, Lady Clara and Adele, standing in the doorway of the women's sleeping room. Ysabel wondered if they were looking for her.

As Adele and Lady Clara disappeared into the room, a group of laundry maids poured through the doorway leading from the basement laundry rooms. Ysabel retied the leather strings on her waistbag, looking busy as the maids walked past her toward the servants' hall where they would eat their midday meal. Their red hands and sturdy arms glistened with the sheep fat they rubbed on their skin to soothe it after their morning's work of washing the castle linen in tubs of hot water and harsh lye soap.

A man called for more ale, startling Ysabel. She looked at the door to the women's hall. Lady Clara was still inside with Adele. She drummed her fingers against the pillar, worried that she could not enter the room to retrieve her cloak without being discovered. She knew Lady Clara and Adele would be concerned about her, believing she was frightened after her sister had been locked up. They would try to keep her out of sight of the queen until the baby princess was returned and Olenna was freed. But Ysabel couldn't hide for the next six days; she had to rescue the child from the Anthra.

From the kitchen passageway, two girls appeared carrying trays of bread and cheese toward the stairs leading to the queen's rooms. Ysabel left the pillar and followed the girls up the stairwell. They ignored her as they whispered to each other, wondering if the giant bird would eat the baby herself or save her for her chicks. Both declared they would not fetch water from the outside wells until the princess or her bones were recovered. The girls quieted when they reached the door to the queen's chambers. Ysabel waited until they stepped inside the room, then rushed up the next flight of stairs to the nurseries where the young children of the castle slept and played. The floor was deserted. The children and their maids were at their midday meal in a room at the far end of the hall. Behind a partly open door, Ysabel heard a woman quietly singing to soothe a crying baby.

Ysabel entered Blane and Rowen's room. She stepped over an army of painted wooden soldiers scattered across the floor and walked through an archway at the end of the room into the baby's nursery. Lira's white cradle was placed next to Olenna's neatly made bed. Ysabel looked around the room and spied her sister's old boots tossed in a corner. She took off her shoes and pulled on the leather boots. Her toes were slightly cramped, but the leather would stretch as she walked and the thicker soles would keep her feet warm. She picked up Olenna's wool cloak from the foot of her bed. A darker imprint of a curling design down the front of the garment showed where gold thread had been picked out of the fine blue wool before it was passed down from one of the queen's ladies to the wet nurse.

She bundled the cloak under her arm and ran down the stairs, through the noise of the great hall, and into the passageway leading to the kitchen. She walked past the cooks sitting around the chopping table with their big knives close to hand, drinking ale and stuffing their mouths with chunks of meat and cheese, eating quickly before they started preparing the evening meal. At the counter, the little sparrows clung to the bars of their cage, watching a kitchen girl pour steaming water into the big clay pot.

Ysabel paused outside the kitchen door and looked across the courtyard at the horse stables. The journey was too far for her to go on foot. She needed a horse, but she couldn't take one of the king's hunters; they were too big and spirited. She remembered an old mare that was kept in a stall at the back of the stables. The little horse was rarely used and might not be missed until Ysabel was far away from the castle.

Next to the stables, the smith's awning was pulled down. The big smith and the stable master were sitting with the fruit pickers under a tree, eating their meal of bread and apples. No one paid heed to Ysabel as she darted across the courtyard toward the stables.

She picked a wrinkled apple from a bucket inside the door. Tall horses with shiny eyes stared at her as she walked down the row of wooden stalls. One horse stood in the stall at the far end, the fat old mare that every child in the castle first learned to ride. Ysabel fed the apple to the horse, unhooked a halter from the wall and placed it on the old mare's head.

"There you are."

Ysabel whirled around to see Adele standing behind her with her hand on her hip.

"What are you doing, Ysabel? Lady Clara is worried. We've been all over the castle looking for you."

"I'm leaving. I have to try and find Princess Lira and save my sister."

"You can't go alone, you don't even know how to ride a horse. Wait for the king, he'll recover the baby."

Ysabel looked at her friend. "King Jeramin is far away and no one believes he'll find her in time. And you heard what the queen said; she'll send Olenna and Blane to work as slaves in her father's mines if Princess Lira does not come home. Do you know what that means, Adele? They'll break rocks and haul ore all day. My sister is a woman, not a strong man, and Blane is a little boy; they won't last long in the mines."

"What are you going to do?"

Ysabel buckled the halter on the little mare's neck. "I'm going to find the canyons where the Anthra has her nest and rescue the princess."

"But why are you looking for her in the canyons? The guards say the bird flew with the baby to the land of the giants."

"I can't go everywhere." Ysabel tightened the halter strap. "Madron's old granddad said the Anthra nests in the canyons. She told me to talk with Daniel the leathermaker. He said I could reach the canyons faster if I travel through the Darkmaren Forest and across the Empty Valley, so that's where I'm going."

She stopped and looked at Adele. "Come with me. We could take another horse and ride together."

"I wish I could, but I'm going home soon to prepare for my wedding. My father and mother would be very angry with me and with Lady Clara if I did not return home."

The girls were silent for a moment. Ysabel turned to the horse and gathered the reins. "I have to leave. Tell Olenna I will come back as soon as I can."

"Wait. Do you have food?"

"I have a piece of bread."

"I'll fetch something for you. Don't leave until I come back."

"Find a knife for me in the kitchen. All I have for protection is my scissors."

Adele ran from the stables while Ysabel led the old horse along the row of stalls to the open door. People under the trees had finished their meals and were napping in the shade. Across the courtyard, one of the cooks stepped out of the kitchen and sat on Daniel's bench and fanned his red face with his hand.

Ysabel patted the mare's warm neck, anxious to be away from the castle. The mare was old and worn out, but she belonged to King Jeramin. Ysabel wondered what would happen if the guards stopped her for taking the horse. Would she be judged a thief and sent to work in the silver mines with Olenna?

People under the trees began to stir. The red-faced cook put his hands on his knees and heaved up from the bench. As he entered the kitchen, Adele slid past him with a cloth napkin in her hand. She ran across the yard toward Ysabel. "Here," she said. "I brought a piece of cheese and a chicken leg. The cooks are working in the kitchen. I couldn't take a knife without them seeing me."

The cheese and chicken leg weren't much, but Ysabel thought she could find nuts and berries to eat while she traveled through the woods. The lack of a knife worried her. She would have to sharpen a stout stick and use it, along with her scissors, if she had to fight the Anthra.

Ysabel tucked the end of the napkin under her belt and grasped the reins. Adele pointed to the top of the castle where two guards had stopped to talk before continuing their rounds along the castle walk. "Put on the blue cloak," she said. "I'll walk with you and it will look as if I'm accompanying one of the queen's ladies on her ride."

She followed Ysabel, leading the mare. When they reached the small gate, the doors to the great hall swung open. They heard men laughing inside the hall as they left the table after their meal. Adele looked up to make sure the guards were not in sight, pulled the pole from the iron loops and opened the gate.

The girls hugged. Adele kissed Ysabel on her cheek. "Return safely, my friend."

She closed the wooden gate. Ysabel heard the bolt slide through the rings and her friend's footsteps running across the courtyard toward the castle doors.

❧ Five ❧

The road from the entrance gates ran straight toward the foot of Darkmaren Hill before it stopped and split into two roads. A large boulder on the left marked the turn to the villages to the south. On the right, the road led toward villages north of the castle.

The roads were empty while people in the fields took their midday rest. In the days after harvest, the roads would be thronging with villagers bringing baskets of ripe pears and tender berries, barrels of new ale, and jars of wild honey to be sold to the castle or tallied against their yearly obligation to King Jeramin for the use of his forests and lands.

Ysabel remembered walking along the road with her sister the year before, proudly bearing a basket of wool spun by their mother. "Fine enough for the queen's gowns," Olenna said as they waited to appear before the head weaver. The wool had been well received and they returned to the cottage with a

handful of copper coins, enough money to add a separate
sleeping room for Olenna and her family. They had planned to
build after the summer haymaking, but baby Emma and
Robert died before the grasses were tall enough for the scythe
and the room had not been built.

Ysabel held onto the bridle and jumped up at the little
mare's back. Her arms and hands slid off the short, rough hair
and she fell to the ground, smacking her elbow. The horse
looked down at her and twitched her tail. Ysabel untangled the
cloak around her legs, picked up the reins and led the horse to
a flat rock at the side of the road. She stepped on the rock,
grabbed a handful of coarse mane and pulled herself up and
onto the mare's broad back. The horse flicked her ears when
Ysabel kicked her high on her ribs. She kicked her again. The
old mare tossed her head, trotted a few quick steps and slowed
to a steady walk.

Wheat fields spread out on either side of the road. In the
distance, a few cows wandered over a fallow strip, dropping
dung onto the unturned soil. A boy followed them, flicking
their bony sides with a long stick when they veered toward the
ripe wheat.

Ysabel was impatient at the slow pace of the horse. She
wanted to kick the mare into a gallop and fly across the fields.
She thought about her journey. She would follow the old
leathermaker's directions and cut through the Darkmaren
Forest and the Empty Valley. If she kept going, stopping only
to feed and rest the horse, she might reach the canyons in two

days. She could be home again in another couple of days, long before the six days granted by the queen had passed.

She rode for a few minutes, wondering how she would wrest the princess from the Anthra's claws. She shuddered, remembering the bird slamming into her back and the iron hard grip of its talons. She felt for the scissors in her waistbag, wishing she had been able to steal one of the cook's long knives.

When Ysabel had ridden halfway to the hill, a herd of sheep rounded the big marker rock, heading toward the castle. A string of bells tied around the neck of the lead sheep rang out, a cheerful sound in the hot afternoon. Ysabel steered her horse a few steps into the wheat to let the black-eared sheep move along the road. The shepherd touched his hat to her as he walked past.

Ysabel turned toward the hill again. She heard someone calling her name and looked back to see Daniel riding up the road, waving his hat with his cloak flapping behind him. She kicked her horse. The mare whinnied at her stable mate and refused to move.

The old man rode around the sheep and stopped in front of Ysabel. "I saw you and your friend at the gate. Where are you going?" His forehead was creased with wrinkles. "Do you know the punishment for stealing the king's horse?"

She tightened her grip on the reins. "No one rides this old mare. I need a horse so I can save Princess Lira and free my sister."

"And how will you do that?"

"As you said, I'll travel through the Darkmaren Forest to the canyons."

"You go on a fool's errand, my girl. Come back with me. I told the stable master we were putting the horses to exercise. He won't look for them for an hour or so."

"No, I won't go back. You can send the guards after me." Ysabel pulled on the reins, but her horse would not move. "Then I'll walk." She slid off the mare and threw the reins over her back. "Take your stupid horse back to the castle."

Daniel laughed as he reached for the reins. "You possess a mighty will for a small girl. Don't be foolish, come back to the castle and wait for King Jeramin to find his child."

"My sister and her son will be on a slave ship to Wymerin before he returns." Ysabel turned to walk up the road and bumped into an old woman carrying a brown and white goose. The bird slipped from the woman's grasp and fled into the wheat, holding up its wings like curved arms.

"My goose, my goose," cried the woman. "Catch my goose."

Ysabel ran after the bird. She was deep in the wheat when she caught up to the goose that had stopped to eat a mouthful of grain. The goose hissed and flapped its wings at her. She kicked at it until the bird jumped backwards. Ysabel rushed forward, grabbed it and wrapped her arm around its plump body. The goose bit her hand. Ysabel yelled and slapped its hard beak, wanting to wring its neck. She carried the bird, honking and kicking its black webbed feet, back to the old woman standing in the road.

Daniel sat on his horse, grinning at Ysabel's struggles with the goose.

"Bless you," said the old woman when Ysabel gained the road. "He is a rascal." Her eyes were very blue in her wrinkled face. "What is your name, child."

"Ysabel."

"Ah, Ysabel, you are a good girl, let me repay you." She reached into her waistbag and pulled out a large bundle of undyed linen. She slowly opened the cloth, corner by corner. Inside lay a grey river rock, pointed at one end. The woman handed the bundle to Ysabel and lifted her goose from Ysabel's arms.

Ysabel held the rock, feeling cheated. A worn copper coin she would have refused, a gift of bread she would have welcomed, but a rock tucked inside a piece of old linen seemed worthless.

The goose woman smiled and Ysabel felt a breeze gently tug her hair. "You will find my gifts useful." She cocked her head and studied Ysabel. "You wear a blue cloak. Are you one of the queen's ladies out on a ride with your groom?"

Ysabel smiled when Daniel frowned at being called her groom.

"I am on a journey, good woman." She hesitated, wondering if she should tell the old woman her plans.

"A journey? To one of the villages, perhaps?"

"No, to a faraway place. My sister Olenna is wet nurse to Princess Lira who was taken by a giant bird this morning." The old woman nodded as if she had heard of the abduction of the baby princess.

Ysabel continued. "King Jeramin and his men are away on a long hunt and will not have enough time to rescue the princess. Queen Ceradona holds my sister accountable because the baby was in her care. She has vowed to send Olenna to work in her father's silver mines if Princess Lira does not return unharmed. My sister would not survive the mines. I must find the baby and save Olenna."

"You have made an excellent start." The old woman leaned closer to Ysabel. "Are you afraid of snakes like many silly girls?" she asked. "Do you scream at spiders?"

"No."

"Good. They may help or hinder, but they have their place." She hitched up the goose in her arms. "Now you must hurry, Princess Lira waits for you."

Ysabel suddenly felt tired at the thought of walking up Darkmaren Hill. "I can't make this journey alone," she said. "It's a long way to travel and now I have no horse."

"I see two horses and a stouthearted man at your side; everything else will come when it is needed."

Daniel held up his hand. "These are King Jeramin's horses. I'm taking them back to the stables before they're missed."

The old woman looked steadily at him. "You must protect this girl. She is in need of your strong arm."

Daniel scratched his beard and nodded at the goose woman's request. Ysabel thought he looked pleased at her words. Likely no one had called him stouthearted or strong for a long time.

"I'll accompany her a short way," he said.

"Go with her as far as you can." The goose woman hitched her bird up higher in her arms and said, "Now be off."

The goose laid his head on her shoulder and gazed at Daniel and Ysabel as the old woman walked down the road toward the castle.

Ysabel retied the strings of Olenna's cloak around her neck and stepped back on the road. She wanted to mount the old mare but feared Daniel would keep the reins and lead the horse back to the castle. She started walking toward Darkmaren Hill.

"You'll not make it through the forest before nightfall," Daniel said. "You'll sleep rough and alone in the dark." He paused. "I believe smallbears still roam those woods. They would make a quick meal of you."

Ysabel turned and yelled, "Go back to your bench. Leave me alone. I don't need you."

Daniel's forehead wrinkled again as he sighed. He clicked his tongue at his horse and rode up to Ysabel. "You are foolish but determined," he said. "I'll escort you through the forest, then take the horses back to the stable."

He leaned down and offered his hand. Ysabel wanted to refuse, but there were no rocks nearby for her to stand upon to mount her horse.

"I will not wait for you to accept," the old man said. At Ysabel's nod, he grabbed her arm and pulled her up until she could sling her leg over the mare's back.

At the crest of the hill, they looked back at the countryside. Strips of yellow wheat and the grassy fallow fields covered the land up to the gates of the castle. Inside the thick walls, thatched roofs of the outbuildings appeared as brown rectangles. Beyond the castle lay the glimmering waters of the Drandelon Sea. Black spots on the water were boats of fishermen returning with their morning catch. Two bigger shapes, trading ships, floated inside the narrow harbor.

Ysabel gazed at her village, a cluster of cottages separated from the castle by wheat fields. She wondered what her friends would say when they heard that Olenna was imprisoned in the tower and Ysabel had stolen one of the king's horses and ridden away.

Daniel pointed to the wheat closest to the castle. "Those fields will be surrounded by walls next year. The steward has persuaded King Jeramin to build a market place there to attract foreign merchants. The harbor will be made bigger to accommodate their ships. Soon there will be a town where you see wheat."

"The villagers need those fields," Ysabel said. "If the king takes them away, we will not have enough wheat and barley to trade or to feed us through winter."

"There will be plenty for all. The forests at the edge of the fields will be cut down to open more land for the plow. A bigger harbor means more ships and new goods in the marketplace. This kingdom is growing, my child."

"That will make Queen Ceradona happy."

"It will. She remembers her father's rich kingdom. King Jeramin is a different ruler, his heart is in the hunt, but he is fortunate in his steward. John Cauldgate will make him a wealthy king."

Ysabel pulled the reins, turning her horse toward the forest. "I don't care about riches while my sister is locked in the tower. Come now, your words waste time."

Wild summer growth blocked the path into the Darkmaren Forest. Daniel led Ysabel through prickly bushes dotted with white flowers and around the trunks of immense trees. Bands of shadow and sunlight slid over her arms as she breathed the cool air. Far above their heads, small birds twittered and cheeped in their nests. Black crows stood on branches and cawed at their passing.

Daniel halted near a stream bubbling with clear water. He slid off his horse and handed the reins to Ysabel. "Water the horses and we will be on our way."

She dismounted as he limped over to a tree and sat with his back against the trunk. He was rubbing his leg when Ysabel led the horses to the stream. He was asleep a few minutes later when she returned.

Ysabel watched him snoring in the sun. He is old and lame, she thought. He would slow her down. She tied his horse to a bush, stepped up on a stump and mounted the mare. They followed the stream deeper into the forest. Ysabel chewed her bread and cheese and gnawed the chicken leg as she rode. Several times she felt someone watching her and turned around, expecting to see Daniel riding after her. She saw a wall of green trees and nothing more.

ᚨ Six ᚱ

The forest thinned as Ysabel rode downhill toward the Empty Valley. She was hungry and her legs ached from riding the broadbacked old mare, but she was relieved she no longer had to worry about Daniel returning the horse to the stable.

She halted at the tree line to view the countryside below. The late afternoon sun slanted across a flat land scraped bare of grass and trees, without a glint of water. A dirt road no wider than a footpath was scratched across the dry land. A lone cottage stood by the road at the far end of the valley.

"Muck and mire," she muttered and sank her forehead into her mare's bristly mane. Beyond the valley, another mountain waited to be crossed.

The sun was halfway down the sky when Ysabel arrived at the little house. She slid off the mare, tied her to a stone post and stumbled on stiff legs up the path, past a stack of firewood. An old woman opened the door before Ysabel raised her hand to knock. The woman's back was bent under her loose wool dress. Her white hair hung in a thin braid down her back.

She stretched her wrinkled neck to look past Ysabel at the road. "All alone, my girl? What do you want?"

"Good day to you," Ysabel said. "I am hungry and beg to work for a piece of bread."

The old woman smiled, showing yellow stubs of teeth. Her eyes were small, like polished black seeds. "I have no work, but you are welcome to stop here. I take in anyone who knocks at my door."

She pointed to a wooden bucket perched on a log in the woodpile. "Take your horse to the barn. Give her hay and water from my well. Come to the side door when you're finished and I'll feed you."

Behind the cottage, Ysabel hauled up water from a moss-lined hole in the ground. She led her horse through a door sagging on its hinges into a small shed. A wooden trough stood against the back wall. A mound of musty smelling hay was heaped on the ground next to the door.

The mare had eaten a mouthful of hay and was noisily drinking from the bucket when Ysabel walked back to the cottage and knocked on the side door. At the old woman's shout, she entered the kitchen.

The woman stood at a table next to the warm hearth, slicing a round of brown bread. "Eat, drink," she said and pointed to a wooden bowl of soup and a cup of water placed on the table.

Ysabel sat on the one stool and took her wooden spoon from her waistbag. The turnip soup was a little watery she thought, not like her mother's thick soups. Her eyes wandered around the kitchen as she ate. Netted bags holding something dark and wrinkled hung from hooks on the wall. Ysabel remembered Olenna's husband, Robert, suspending the hind leg of their newly slaughtered pig from the rafter above the kitchen hearth to hang for two months, slowing curing in the smoke from the cookfire until the start of the winter festival.

On the morning of the festival, Robert cut the ham from the rafter and laid it on the table where her mother waited with her sharpened knife. Ysabel sat on a stool holding Blane and watched her mother slice through the blackened skin, revealing the pink flesh inside. Ysabel licked her lips, remembering the taste of the delicious, salty meat.

The clunk of the old woman's knife on the table brought Ysabel out of her memories. "Do you live here alone?" she asked.

"Yes," said the woman as she handed Ysabel a piece of bread. "My family scattered to the winds long ago."

"Aren't you lonely?"

"Enough people travel through the valley to give me company," the old woman said. "Though none as young as you."

She leaned over the table. "There is something caught in your hair." She plucked a faded white flower from Ysabel's head, pulling out several red hairs.

"Ouch." Ysabel rubbed her head. "That hurt."

"All out." The woman dropped the flower on a shelf above the hearth.

Ysabel reached for the cup of water. "I was traveling with an old man but he fell asleep and I had to leave him in the forest." She held the cup to her lips and put it down again when she heard her mare whinny, a high, quick sound.

"Your horse is still hungry," said the woman. "Give her more hay. Make a bed of it for yourself if you wish to stay the night."

Ysabel drank a few sips of water as she walked across the yard. Her feet felt heavier with each step. She yawned so wide she thought her jaw would crack. She wanted nothing more than to lie down on the hay and sleep until morning.

The horse stood with her head in the empty trough. The bucket at her feet was kicked over and a dark patch showed where water had soaked into the dirt. Ysabel set her cup on the ground and leaned against the mare, barely able to lift her hand to pat her neck.

"Wake up," she said, yawning. "We have to leave."

The horse did not twitch at Ysabel's touch. She pushed against the mare's head. It felt as if it was glued to the trough. She picked up the bucket, hoping the horse would wake at the smell of fresh water. She glanced inside. In the bit of water left at the bottom, an image of the mare stared at her with wide-open eyes. Ysabel cried out at the strange picture and dropped the bucket. She stepped away from the overturned bucket and looked at the cup on the ground. Water in the cup shone like a little mirror. She leaned over it and saw the bottom of the wooden cup. Her face was not reflected in the water. She jerked away as the hairs rose on the back of her neck.

Ysabel had not heard tales of well water that could enthrall a horse into a deep sleep or hide a reflection. Her mother had told her stories about little fairies that lived in the flower garden and wore rose petals for dresses, and warned her about marsh lights that appeared over swampy water in the woods. The lights were the breath of people who had died in the marsh, her mother said. They were lonely and used the wispy white lights to lure travelers from the path into the sucking mud. There they would drown and become companions to the marsh ghosts.

Ysabel had looked under every petal when she was a little girl, hoping to see a fairy. She never did, but she had seen a soft ball of white light once when she was late returning from the woods. The floating light seemed to beckon her to come closer, deeper into the marsh. As Ysabel took a step off the path into cold, squishy mud, she remembered her mother's warning. She had turned her eyes from the light and ran as fast as she could until she was out of the woods.

The sound of a horse trotting up the road brought Ysabel to the shed door. Daniel had stopped in front of the cottage and was dismounting from his horse. She wanted to run to him but held back, worried he would be angry with her for taking the king's horse and leaving him asleep in the forest.

The old woman appeared in the doorway as Daniel tied his horse to the post. He limped up the path, pulled off his hat and bowed to her. He held his hand up to the height of his shoulder and pointed back toward the Darkmaren Hill.

He was asking about her, thought Ysabel. Daniel dropped his hand when the woman shook her head. She spoke to him as he turned to leave. He nodded and walked to the woodpile, gathered an armload of wood and carried it into the cottage.

Ysabel heard the door close behind him. "She told him I'm not here," she said aloud. "Why does she conceal me?"

She waited in the doorway for Daniel to reappear, running once to the mare to stroke her neck, trying to rouse her from her sleep and back again to stand at the door. Her stomach growled at the smell of a pie baking in the kitchen. The old woman was feeding Daniel. Perhaps he would be in a good mood to see Ysabel after he ate and not be angry that she had ridden on without him.

She started across the yard and jumped back into the shed when the kitchen door opened. The old woman stepped outside into the light of sunset, carrying a lacy white shawl over her arm. She looked taller, her back no longer bent. A veil of black silk was draped over her hair. She had changed her clothing from the shapeless wool garment to a fitted green dress that was embroidered all over with twisting black vines.

Daniel's horse shied from her when she untied him from the fence. The white shawl fell to the ground as the old woman fought to control the horse. He reared up, tearing the leads from her hands. He shook himself free and galloped away from the cottage and down the road toward Darkmaren Hill.

The woman bent to pick up the shawl. The black silk slipped from her head as she straightened up, revealing her hair that had turned deep red and fell thick and loose over her shoulders. She covered her hair again and walked toward the shed, shaking out the lacy shawl.

Ysabel backed away from the door, frightened by the change in the old woman. She stumbled over the cup on the ground. She picked it up and tossed the water into a dark corner, not wanting the woman to know that she had not drunk all the water. The woman was coming closer. Ysabel dropped the cup on the ground and quickly lay down on the hay with her face turned toward the wall.

"Good girl," the woman said as she entered the room. Her voice was deeper. Ysabel wondered if she was talking to her or the mare. She knelt beside Ysabel, who breathed slowly, pretending to be asleep. The woman spread the shawl over Ysabel's body, from her legs to her shoulder. She patted her shoulder, saying, "Sleep well, child, I'll bring bread and cakes for you in the morning."

She picked up the bucket and the cup and left the shed. Ysabel waited to move until she heard the cottage door bang shut. The shawl tightened around her shoulders as she rolled over, away from the wall. She poked her fingers through the lace to push it off. The shawl adhered to her hand. She took a deep breath and gently wiggled her leg. Every movement made the lace cling tighter.

"Help," she cried, hoping Daniel would hear her. Yarn in the shawl grasped her throat. She tried to calm herself with shallow breaths while she listened in vain for Daniel's voice or his footsteps hurrying across the yard to the shed.

Should she try to scream again? Would her shouting bring the old woman back to the shed? Ysabel pictured the woman's bright black eyes watching as she struggled to free herself.

Why had the woman bound her? Ysabel's heart banged in her chest as she thought of the netted meats hanging on the kitchen wall. Were those the remains of other travelers she had caught? Was that what the old woman planned for her? And what about Daniel? Was he lying helpless in the cottage, trapped under another shawl?

Ysabel moved her eyes, looking for an axe or a scythe, anything sharp nearby that she could quickly roll against and cut the shawl apart, but there were no tools to be seen, only her mare asleep in front of the trough. And no mice, she realized. There were no black droppings trailing on the ground. Nothing moved in the quiet shed. No lice crawled over her as she lay in the rotten hay, no flies buzzed around the horse.

Her left arm was tucked under her side and untouched by the shawl. She slowly moved her hand until she grasped the bottom of her waistbag and pulled it down. She worked her hand inside the bag and hooked her finger through the loop of her scissors, careful not to disturb the shawl. As she drew out the blades, the scissors fell off her finger and down into the hay.

"Eye of pig," she whispered, wanting to yell her frustration.

She moved her fingers through the hay until she felt a hard metal tip, pinched it and lifted the scissors. She pried open the blades and pressed one sharp edge against the shawl over her thigh. The yarns parted. She kept cutting it, thread by thread, from her leg to her waist. The shawl lost power as she cut it. The yarn was limp around her throat when she finally sliced through the last threads.

Ysabel brushed the severed yarn from her body, got to her feet and ran to the doorway. The first stars of evening had appeared. Across the yard, a lit candle in the kitchen threw an array of yellow light through the shuttered window. The kitchen went dark. A few minutes later, a light glowed in an upper room before it was blown out.

She had to wait until the woman was asleep. She counted to one hundred as she tied her cloak strings, counted again and then ran across the yard to stand with her ear against the door. She listened for the sound of voices. The house was silent.

Ysabel opened the door and stepped into the warm room. A plate with half a pie was set in the middle of the table. She heard a man snoring and saw Daniel wrapped snug in his cloak, sleeping on a straw pallet close to the smoking hearth.

Ysabel listened for the old woman, but heard only Daniel, grunting and wheezing in his sleep. She knelt beside the pallet and shook his arm. He snored louder. She shook him again.

"Wake up," she whispered.

He opened his eyes. "Ysabel, is that you?" He sat up, yawning. "Where have you been?"

"Shh, be quiet. Get up, we have to leave."

Daniel rubbed his stomach and looked around the room. "I'm hungry. Where is the old woman? She said she would feed me if I brought in more wood."

"If you eat her food again, you'll never leave this house." Ysabel looked at the row of netted meats hanging above her on the wall. "She had horrible plans for us."

Moonlight pushed through the window. Ysabel heard a slithering sound overhead, as if a silk coverlet was sliding off a bed. "Hurry, she is waking up."

She pulled him up and dragged him by the hand toward the open door.

"Ah, apple pie." Daniel reached for the plate on the table.

"No." She slapped his hand. "Do not eat her food."

As they moved toward the door, she saw a wooden comb on a shelf. Three white hairs, kinked from being braided, were caught in its teeth. She picked the hairs out of the comb. They twisted in her fingers, forming a thick fuzzy knot.

"You took my hair," Ysabel muttered and dropped the knot into her waistbag.

She heard the thump of feet hitting the floor in the upper room and a long, scraping sound. "Go," she said and shoved Daniel out of the house.

"Where are the horses?" he asked as they ran onto the road.

"Your horse ran away and my mare is deep asleep. She drank water from the old woman's well and will not wake up." Ysabel grabbed Daniel's hand. "Come, we must hurry from this place."

After a few minutes, Daniel stopped to rub his leg. The moon was a hand above the edge the valley, flooding the barren land with white light. The smell of freshly baked bread floated toward them.

Daniel held his stomach, groaning, "I'm hungry."

"Me, too, but keep moving." The old woman was trying to lure them back. Ysabel walked faster, remembering the dark meats hanging on the kitchen wall and the lace shawl tightening around her throat.

"She is a good cook," Daniel said as he limped after Ysabel. "She made lamb stew for me and baked an apple pie. Her food was so good I ate until I thought I would burst, but as soon as I stopped eating I was hungry again."

"Didn't you see that she became younger while you were eating?" The old woman's hair had turned red and she changed her dress. How had he missed that?

"I didn't notice." Daniel shrugged. "I drank a lot of ale."

The smell of roasting meat followed them, so rich that Ysabel tasted crispy, salted fat on her tongue and Daniel cried out, as if in pain. When they reached the first boulders at the foot of the mountain, the scent of food disappeared. Ysabel led the way up the steep mountainside in the moonlight, scrambling over loose rocky soil and grabbing handfuls of the scraggy bushes to pull herself up. Behind her, Daniel grumbled at her pace. She ignored his panted requests to rest and did not stop moving until dawn, when they reached the top of the mountain.

The stars were fading in the pale sky. The valley was filled with the cold blue light of early morning. One moment Ysabel thought she saw the little house by the road, the next moment it was not there.

"We walked all night. I have to ease my leg." Daniel lowered himself to the ground, wincing at the pain in his leg.

"You slept earlier, we can't stop."

Daniel leaned against a rock and closed his eyes.

"Why did you come after me?" Ysabel said.

"I had to return the king's horses."

She crossed her arms. "Go back and fetch my horse if you want it so badly. The old woman will be happy to see you. She'll bake another pie for you."

Daniel laughed. "I am not that hungry, my girl." He opened his eyes and looked at Ysabel. "You saved me from her evil plans. I am in your debt and will accompany you however far you wish to travel."

"I thought you were angry with me because I left you asleep in the woods."

"I was surprised that you were so bold as to ride through the forest alone. When the old woman said she had not seen you, I feared your horse had thrown you into a ravine. I meant to ride back and search for you, but I was hungry and she offered to feed me if I fetched wood for her fire. She made a good meal and I ate and could not stop eating. Then I was so tired I could not keep my eyes open."

"You ate well. I think she was fattening you up to eat you."

Daniel patted his round belly. "She wouldn't have to fatten me very much. I have plenty here."

"I'm hungry," Ysabel said. "The old woman gave me a bowl of soup that tasted like water. Mayhap she was saving me for later."

"We'll look for food tomorrow. For now, sleep with your hand pressed against your belly and you'll feel less hungry." He yawned, making Ysabel yawn.

"Take your rest," she said. "We'll start again soon."

She wrapped her cloak around her, covering her arms and legs against the cold. She thought of Daniel's advice and pressed her fist into her stomach. She didn't feel as hungry, but she was thirsty and her feet ached inside Olenna's heavy boots. She sat up and brushed away a rock that was poking into her shoulder. She lay down again and closed her eyes.

⚜ Seven ⚜

Ysabel woke with the sun in her eyes. She blinked as a shadow fell over her and looked up to see Daniel standing above her with his knife in his hand. He raised the blade, saying, "Don't move, Ysabel."

She held her breath, shocked at the sight of Daniel and his upraised knife. Why did he want to hurt her? She tensed her body, ready to roll away from the blade when his eyes moved to look at the rock next to her. She heard a hissing sound and slowly turned her head. A bronze-colored snake was uncoiling its long body from the rock, rising in the air from its resting place on the sun-warmed stone.

A drop of clear venom hung from one of its sharp fangs. Ysabel let out her breath as the snake looked down at her with its yellow eyes. The snake flicked its forked tongue, tasting her scent in the air as it moved its body back and forth, back and forth. Ysabel felt drowsy as she watched the snake swaying in front of her.

The snake paused, then struck. Daniel was ready; as soon as the snake moved, he swung his knife down and sliced off its head. The body dropped in a heap. The head bounced off the rock, ringing like a bell. Ysabel screamed as it hit the ground. She jumped up and stood behind Daniel, watching the head roll to a stop where she had been sleeping. The body of the snake unwound and slid off the back of the rock in a smear of dark blood.

Ysabel clutched Daniel's arm, her teeth chattering with fear. "It was going to bite me." She let go of his arm. "Did you hear it? The head sounded like a bell."

The bronze-colored scales gleamed in the sunlight and were closely lapped, like the armor of a wealthy knight. Daniel poked the snakehead with his knife. The eyes did not open.

"Pick it up," Ysabel said. "The goose woman said snakes were pests, remember? But she said they had their uses. We should take the head. It may help us on our journey."

Daniel impaled the head on the tip of his knife and held it toward Ysabel. "Open your waistbag."

She shook her head, "No, you killed it, you carry it."

Daniel sighed, wiped the blood from the neck on the grass and slid the snake's head into his belt pouch.

Ysabel followed him around the rocks and down into a grass meadow, a shallow bowl on top of the mountain. The bowl was rimmed with black-limbed trees that were bent over and twisted from the constant wind. Sunlight warmed their shoulders as they walked along the bottom of the bowl. Daniel was limping again. Ysabel wanted to tell him to walk faster; she was anxious to reach the far side and see how much farther they had to travel before they reached the canyons of the Anthra. But Daniel had saved her from the snake and she did not want to shame him by running ahead, leaving him to catch up with her.

They were in the center of the bowl when she heard a rustling sound. She turned to see the bronze body of the headless snake winding though the grass behind her. Daniel yelled and stumbled backward. He held his waistbag away from his body. One of the fangs of the snake's head had poked through the pouch. Ysabel screamed as the second fang tore through the leather.

"What do we do?" she cried. "You cut off its head, yet it lives."

"We should give it back." Daniel untied his pouch, keeping his fingers away from the sharp fangs.

"No, no, the head sounded a bell for us. We have to keep it."

As she spoke, the grass around them shook as if they were surrounded by hundreds of serpents. The air buzzed with their hissing.

"We're trapped," Daniel shouted. He reached inside the pouch to retrieve the head.

"Wait." Ysabel jerked open her waistbag and felt the stuffed lamb under her fingers. She grabbed the wool. "This might work," she said, and flung the toy at the headless snake.

The hissing serpents fell silent. Ysabel heard a little bleat as the lamb flew through the air. The sound surprised her. She thought it must have been the wind through the trees.

The headless body of the snake coiled around the bit of white wool when it hit the ground. The grass around them stopped shaking, the fangs drew back into the pouch. Daniel and Ysabel ran through the grass, jumping over fallen branches from the wind-bent trees that looked like the twisted forms of black snakes. Were they branches or snakes? wondered Ysabel. She didn't stop to look closely, but kept running until she reached the far side of the meadow.

She ran up the side and stopped at the top, her chest heaving. Daniel hobbled up from the meadow and stood next to her, rubbing his knee.

"How did you know to throw the toy?" he asked.

"I wanted to distract it and threw what I had in my waistbag."

After they caught their breath, they walked to the edge of the mountain and looked down at a dense forest that spread over the land below. The trees ended at the edge of an enormous blue lake. A rough line of sand-colored canyons lay between the lake and a vast body of water stretching across the horizon.

"That's the Sefrit Sea," Daniel said. "The waters at the end of the world. Those canyons must be where the Anthra has her nest."

"It's too far," Ysabel said. "We'll never reach the nest in time."

Daniel pointed to the blue lake. "We would save time if we could cross that lake instead of walking around it to the canyons. Hmm, mayhap we could build a boat."

"We don't have time to make a boat. We would have reached the canyons by now if we had kept our horses, but they're gone and we travel slowly because you're old and lame and have to rest all the time." She was tired of Daniel. Why couldn't one of the younger guards have offered to come with her? The strong looking man who had carried Blane to the tower room would have walked faster. He would have thought of a way to cross the lake.

Daniel replied, "Start running then, if you think you will get there the quicker." He reached out to pat Ysabel's shoulder and pulled back his hand when she glared at him. Daniel shrugged and stepped onto a goat trail. Ysabel wanted to cry as she looked at the distance they had to travel. She would never find the Anthra's nest in time to recover the baby.

"Come on, Ysabel," Daniel called. "Keep up."

She wiped her eyes, retied her cloak and followed him down the mountain.

At midday they entered the forest that was hazy with drifting seeds and insects lazily turning in the slanting sunlight. After a few minutes of walking through silent trees, Daniel stopped and drew his knife.

"I smell bread," he whispered.

Ysabel sniffed the air. Her stomach ached with hunger. "Me, too. Did the old woman follow us?"

"I am ready for her if she did." Daniel continued moving through the woods, pausing every few steps to look around a tree trunk for the old woman.

"Listen," Ysabel said. "Now I hear singing."

It was a deep voice and hollow, as though a man was singing with his hands cupped around his mouth.

"Someone else is in the forest," she said. "Perhaps he'll give us food."

They followed the voice through a thicket of briar bushes. Daniel walked in front of Ysabel, chopping a path through sharp-toothed vines that snagged their clothing and clawed their skin. The bushes grew closer and closer together until Daniel was hacking at a solid wall of thorns. Ysabel pulled out her thread scissors to help him chop through the thorns, but the stems were too thick for her blades.

They were deep inside the brambles when the singing stopped. Ysabel untangled her hair from a wicked looking thorn. "What happened to the voice? Are we lost?"

Daniel looked up at the sky. "I don't think so. If we keep following the sun, we should reach the end of this forest."

"This way is too hard," Ysabel complained. She held out her arms that were bleeding and covered with scratches. "I'm hot and hungry and these thorns are cutting me everywhere. Are you sure this is the way out of the forest?"

He turned around, staring at the mass of thorn bushes surrounding them and shook his head. "No."

The singing started again, turning into a low humming. Daniel renewed slashing through the dense thorns. Ysabel wiped her bloodied arms on her skirt and walked behind him, feeling relieved they weren't alone and eager to meet the unknown man who was leading them through the briars.

The humming sounded closer, beyond the next bush. Daniel carefully pushed aside a clutch of thorns and looked through the bush.

His mouth dropped open.

"What is it?" Ysabel said.

Daniel held up his hand for silence and motioned for her to come closer.

Ysabel stood on tiptoe to look through the opening in the thorns. She took a quick breath and slapped her hand over her mouth. Sitting before her with his back against a tree was an enormous man. His legs were stretched across a cleared area like two felled trees. Even sitting down, he was taller than Daniel. She was looking at a giant! She stepped back. Giants ate humans. He would smell the blood on her arms and come thundering through the bushes, roaring for her flesh.

When nothing happened, she and Daniel looked through the thorns again. The big man's eyes were closed and he was humming as he picked his teeth with a curved white bone.

"That looks like a human rib," Daniel whispered.

"He ate some poor man traveling through the woods," Ysabel said. "We can't go through the clearing. He'll catch us and kill us for his supper."

"There is no other way." Daniel pointed his knife at the thorns that had closed behind them, hiding the path. "We cannot go back the way we came, it will take too long. And we might get trapped in more thorn bushes." He took a deep breath. "I will face the giant. I'll fight him while you run past."

Ysabel nodded at his plan. The old man had fought in battles. He could distract the giant long enough for her to escape. It was her idea to rescue the baby; she should be the one to get away.

Daniel raised his knife and lowered it again. "I don't know how to fight a giant. All I have is my knife. I could throw it at his eye. But what if I don't kill him? What if I merely stick him in the eye and make him angry?"

"Hush," Ysabel said, pushing him through the bush. "You have to try." She followed closely behind Daniel, ready to run if the giant seized the old man. Daniel walked into the clearing and stepped on a stick that cracked loudly under his foot. The giant opened his eyes at the sound. Ysabel and Daniel immediately stopped walking.

"Huh?" said the giant man. He pulled the bone from his mouth, looked at Daniel and Ysabel and smiled. His lips curved full and red under his beard. A small brown bird poked his head through the tangled hair, looked at them for a moment and retreated into the giant's bushy beard.

Daniel raised his knife. "Let us pass. We have no quarrel with you."

The giant's mouth turned down. He sighed and waved the chewed end of the bone at Daniel and Ysabel. "Go, I will not stop you." He spoke slowly. His voice sounded as if it issued from a deep cave.

"But," he waved the bone again at a clay cooking bell nestled in the coals of his cookfire. "I baked fresh bread for my dinner. Stay and eat with me."

"No, we don't eat human flesh," Daniel said.

"I do not eat humans," replied the giant. "I offer you bread and cheese."

"Then why do you pick your teeth with a man's rib?" Daniel pointed his knife at the bone in the giant's hand.

The big man looked at the chewed rib and quickly tossed it behind him, over the treetops. "I found it over there." He pointed a thick finger toward a dark hole dug under a boulder at the end of the clearing.

"It's a bear's den," Daniel said. He walked toward the dark opening with Ysabel close behind him, watching the giant from the corner of her eye. Daniel stopped and looked down at a series of paw marks in the dirt. The wide paws were topped with five toes with a long slash above each toe where the bear's claws had dug into the soft dirt.

"This is the cave of a long-toed bear. It's away now, likely foraging in the woods for a last meal before it begins its winter sleep."

The stink of old blood and rotten flesh hit them when they looked inside the hole. A human skull lay on the ground near the entrance beside a heap of cracked bones. They backed away from the entrance and hit the knee of the giant who stood behind them, bending over to look at the den. Ysabel froze at the touch of his big knee pressed against her back. She stepped closer to Daniel, afraid the giant man might decide to pick her up and stuff her into his mouth.

He didn't move toward her. He continued to speak as though he wanted them to believe he was friendly. "I found the bone in the rocks."

The giant took two steps and was back at his cookfire. He opened an enormous leather satchel and brought out a wooden platter, a round of cheese wrapped in waxed cloth, and several red apples, twice as large as the biggest apples that grew in Liridian.

"I have food." He held out the cheese and apples. "Let me feed you."

Ysabel hesitated. The giant appeared kindly, not a murderous brute that thirsted for her blood. He had welcomed them with an offer of food as her mother had taught her to receive visitors to their cottage. It might be safe to sit for a few minutes and eat his bread and apples. She walked to the end of a log and sat down, leaving Daniel standing between her and the giant.

Daniel sheathed his knife and bowed to the tall man. "We would be honored to join you. I am Daniel, a leathermaker; this girl is Ysabel."

The man bowed in return, bringing his huge head close to Daniel. "I am named Small Horace because I am the smallest giant in my village. My father was Blinker the Giant. My mother is the giantess, Ulsa."

He straightened up. "Now, let me serve you."

Daniel sat beside Ysabel as Horace drew a knife as long as a sword from his belt. He placed one of the apples on the wooden platter and sliced it so finely that sunlight glowed through the yellow flesh. The giant opened his cooking bell and brought out a round of golden bread. He pushed the bell off the coals with his foot to cool and cut the bread into four pieces. He arranged them on the platter, broke off a chunk of cheese and crumbled it over the hot bread. Ysabel thought she would faint at the smell of the melting cheese.

The giant untied a small bag hanging from his belt and sprinkled a pinch of dried green herbs on the bread and cheese. He bowed and presented the platter of food to Daniel and Ysabel.

"I wish I had goose eggs," he said. "I would make a cheese tart for you. But, alas, the bird's eggs in this forest are so small that I cannot gather enough to make a good-sized tart."

Daniel nodded, his mouth full. Ysabel looked at the bread at Horace.

"What did you put on the cheese?" she said.

"Dragon's Tongue. It is plain without it."

Ysabel took a bite. The crust was crunchy, the tangy cheese melted in her mouth, and the Dragon's Tongue added a lick of fire. She smiled at Horace.

"Good, good," the giant said. It sounded like a cow lowing, "Gud, gud."

He reached into his satchel again and pulled out a clay jar and a cup. "Wine from my mother's cellar." He poured red wine into the cup and offered it to Ysabel.

She drew back. "Is it made of blood?" she asked, remembering childhood stories of giants crushing humans with their huge hands to make wine from their blood.

"It's from wild strawberries. I made it for my mother. She liked my wine but she didn't enjoy my cooking because I would not use human flesh. When I was a boy, she stewed a sailing man she caught in the woods. She was angry with me because I did not like the taste of the meat. It was too stringy."

The cup was the size of a large bowl in Ysabel's hands. She sipped the wine. "It tastes like strawberries," she said.

Horace handed the jar to Daniel while Ysabel swallowed another mouthful of the warm sweet wine. She wondered how much human flesh Horace had eaten to know that he did not like the taste of it.

The giant man ate the rest of the bread and two apples. As he chewed, the bird stuck out its head and pecked at bits of food caught in his beard.

When she had finished eating, Ysabel brushed crumbs from her skirt and glanced at Daniel. She tilted her head toward the trees behind Horace. That part of the forest was free of thorn bushes.

Daniel nodded in agreement. "We must leave now," he said and stood, straightening his belt.

Horace stopped chewing and the bird stopped pecking breadcrumbs and they both looked at Daniel and Ysabel.

"I thank you for feeding us," Daniel said. "But we must continue our journey."

"Where are you going in such a hurry?" the giant asked.

"We seek a baby princess who was taken by a great bird called the Anthra," said Ysabel. "We must rescue the baby in two days, before the Anthra feeds her to her hatchlings. If we fail to return the baby three days after the full moon, Queen Ceradona will banish my sister, Olenna, who was wet nurse to the princess. The baby was in her care when the Anthra took her."

"I have heard of those birds," Horace said. "The storywomen in my village talked about them when I was a child. They said the Anthras were big and fierce."

"The Anthra grabbed me when I was holding the princess," said Ysabel. "She lifted me as easily as I would pick up a little baby."

"Let me come with you," Horace said. "I'm small but I'm strong. I'll grab this Anthra and wrestle her to the ground." He picked up a tree branch and snapped it in two pieces. "I'll break her wings and eat her eggs for my morning meal."

When Daniel and Ysabel didn't reply, he dropped the wood and stood over them like a huge child, afraid of being left behind.

"Where is your village? Where is your family?" Daniel asked.

Horace waved his hand toward the south. "My village is two day's walk from here. My father is dead. My mother still lives but she bade me leave our home until I am taller." He looked down at the ground and said in a low voice, "She is ashamed of me because I did not grow as big as my father."

He pointed to the tallest tree surrounding the clearing. "My father was a true giant. He would stand far above that tree."

Ysabel understood feeling like an outcast. She felt like a stranger in her village. The boys ignored her after she had refused their offers to carry her water bucket from the well. Why should she? The well was a few steps from her front door; she didn't need their help. The girls she had grown up with were no different. As children they had played together making mud pies and acorn necklaces. Now they talked of marriage and babies and laughed at Ysabel when she said she'd rather climb the cliffs to gather bird eggs instead of flirting with the village boys.

Horace glanced down at Daniel and Ysabel. "But I have a plan." He reached into the top of his tunic and pulled out a gold chain made of several gold necklaces linked together. "My father left this to me before he died. He had many rings strung on the chain, but my mother kept them. She said I had to find my own gold to wear."

He held up the chain until it glittered in the sunlight. "We giants love gold. I will return to my village bearing bags of gold and everyone will welcome me back."

"Where would you find gold?" Ysabel asked. "Do giants work gold mines? Queen Ceradona's father has silver mines in his country. That's where she threatened to send my sister if we don't save Princess Lira."

Horace shook his big head. "We don't dig for gold; we find it on dead people who wash up on our shore or take it from travelers we capture in the woods." He leaned down and whispered, "I'm going to find the golden tree and pick its leaves."

"Where is this gold tree? I have not heard of it," Daniel said.

"My mother told me stories about it when I was a little boy," said Horace. "The golden tree grows on a small island in the Northfast Sea. Its leaves are pure gold and shine as bright as the sun. Adult giants alone are able to see the golden light and only on the night of the dark moon, after the sea has turned to ice. My mother said that a long time ago, giants tried to reach the island, but they were so heavy that the ice broke under their feet and they drowned in the freezing water."

He pointed toward the north. "I'm a grown giant so I'll see the light and I'm small, the ice won't break under me. I know the way to the Northfast Sea from a traveler my mother had caged in the kitchen. He told me a giant walking five days from my village would reach the Northfast Sea. I've walked for two days, so I'm three days away from the sea. I'll see the gold light and find the tree and fill bags with gold leaves. I'll return to my village and marry Solmay, that's my sweetheart. Her father doesn't like me because I'm poor and small, but he loves gold and will give me his daughter for a bag of gold leaves."

"Are you going to the Northfast Sea now?" Daniel said.

Horace shook his big head. "I was going to stay in these woods where it's warm for a few more days and then walk to the sea." He shuddered. "I don't want to wait there in the cold until the night of the dark moon."

"What happened to the traveler your mother caught?" Ysabel asked. "Did she eat him?"

"I opened the cage and let him escape after he told me how to get to the Northfast Sea. That's another reason my mother is angry with me."

"Let me come with you," he said again. "I don't want to stay here alone. I'll help kill the Anthra and then travel to the Northfast Sea. I'll take one of her feathers and bags of gold back to my village. Everyone will see how rich and brave I am. My mother will welcome me home. I'll marry Solmay and we'll be happy."

He twisted a few of his beard hairs as he waited for their reply.

Ysabel raised her eyebrows at Daniel. "He's strong and he doesn't eat humans," she said in a low voice. "He could help us."

Daniel looked up at the giant who smiled hopefully at him. He turned to Ysabel. "He would be a good companion, he can see farther than we can and he could carry you when you are tired."

"Or you, when your leg hurts," she said.

He ignored her comment. "Come with us, friend," he said to the giant man. "We would welcome your company."

"And your cooking," Ysabel added.

Horace grabbed his clay oven and placed it inside his satchel along with the cup and the wooden platter. He picked up a large axe propped against the tree and shoved it into his belt. He gently pulled the bird from his beard and set it on a branch of the tree.

"Goodbye, little one," he said. "Stay here with your family."

Ysabel and Daniel followed Horace through the trees. The giant walked slowly so they would not have to run to keep up with his every step. He stomped bushes under his big feet and broke off low-lying branches to clear a wide path for them. His large hands swung at his side as he walked, leaning forward as if he was heading into a strong wind.

The giant man looked down at her. "I was glad to see you and Daniel. I do not like being alone during the day or at night."

"But you're so big, Horace. No animal will attack you other than a bear or an ice wolf." Ysabel's neck ached from looking up at Horace.

"There are many small animals with sharp teeth that come out at night, young Ysabel." He stopped, pulled up the sleeve of his shirt and leaned down to show her a mass of red bites around his wrist and up his arm. "They bite quick and run away before I can catch them." He unrolled his sleeve. "I don't like them. I think they will stay away now that I'm traveling with you."

"My neck hurts from looking up at you," Ysabel said. "I don't know why you were called Small Horace, you're very tall to me." She was surprised to discover how comfortable she felt around the giant man. She had forgotten her fear that he wanted to eat her flesh and drink her blood.

Horace raised his arm and pointed over a stand of trees. "I see blue water ahead of us."

"It's a big lake and we have to cross it," Ysabel said. "Beyond it are the canyons of the Anthra."

❧ Eight ☙

The blue lake spread before them, sparkling in the afternoon sun. A steady wind blew across the water, riffling the surface and scattering the brilliant light.

"We need a boat," Daniel said for the third time.

Ysabel rolled her eyes. "We don't have one, Daniel. How many times are you going to say the same thing?"

She glanced up at Horace. "Would you wade into the lake and find out how deep it is? The water might be shallow enough for you to walk across the bottom and pull us after you."

Horace took off his boots and stepped into the lake. He walked slowly until the water was up to his waist. He stopped and lowered himself in the water. After a moment he stood up and came splashing back to shore.

"It drops off," he said. "I knelt down and tried to feel the bottom with my foot, but it was too deep."

He stood on the sand in his wet clothing, twirling a few of his beard hairs into points while he stared at the lake. He suddenly pulled on his boots, took up his axe and went striding into the forest. Ysabel and Daniel heard a crashing sound and the ground jumped under their feet. Horace reappeared, dragging two large pine trees. Thick vines hung from his neck in a long loop. He dropped the trees and vines near the water.

"We will build a log boat," he said. "My friends and I made them to play in the river when we were boys."

"Good idea," said Daniel. He took out his knife and started trimming small branches from the trees while Horace went back into the forest. He lugged out four more trees, two under each arm. He opened his satchel and brought out a rolled up shirt, dyed a rich red, and handed it to Ysabel. "Use this for a sail."

"Your shirt is too nice to cut up," she said. "Do you have anything else in your satchel we could use?"

"No, take this. Put it to use and make a sail out of it. My sweetheart made this for me to wear to the harvest festival this year, but I don't know when my mother will allow me to come home again."

Ysabel sat on a rock near the lake and cut out the front and back sections of the huge shirt with her scissors. She took out thread and a bone needle and began to sew the pieces together. "Muck and mire," she muttered when she stabbed her finger. She disliked sewing, but Horace had asked her to help and she had to do something while he and Daniel built the raft.

Horace chopped off the muddy root balls and the tops of the logs to make them roughly of equal length. He took his axe to the thicker branches while Daniel untangled the vines. When the logs were trimmed, Horace laid four of them in a row and tied them together with lengths of the vines.

Ysabel's hands slowed as she watched the men. She remembered Lady Clara saying, "Don't be in a rush, Ysabel. Sew carefully the first time instead of sewing it again later." She took smaller stitches, tugging on her seams as she worked to tighten her stitches. When she was finished, she knotted the thread and held up the gigantic square of cloth. Her seams were crooked but they were strong. The sail would hold against the wind. They would fly across the water.

Horace tied on the last two logs, one each across the top end of the raft to make it rigid. He stood up, brushing dirt from his knees. "This will do," he said in his deep voice. "It's big enough for me to sit on and looks sturdy enough to hold all of us."

Ysabel handed the cut off sleeves to the giant. "These are all that are left of your shirt."

Daniel opened his belt pouch and pulled out a ball of leather cord. He sliced off a length of cording and lashed two branches together to make a mast and crossbar. He chopped the wood at the bottom of the mast, shaping it into a point and jammed it between two logs at the end of the raft. When he was finished, Ysabel stepped onto the raft and hung one edge of the shirt along the crossbar. She sewed it on with long stitches while Daniel tied the bottom two corners to the outer logs.

The red sail billowed in the evening breeze against the gold and coral sunset. Ysabel pointed to a flock of small green birds swooping over the lake, chasing insects gathered above the cool water. The birds opened their beaks and breathed out short bursts of fire as they raced after their meal. The water roiled when several of the birds flew too close to the lake. Long-jawed fish leapt out of the lake, grabbed the birds and dragged their thrashing bodies under the water.

"I wonder what else is hidden in that lake," Ysabel said.

"We'll cross at dawn," Daniel said, and the others quickly nodded in agreement.

Daniel gathered wood for the fire. Ysabel picked wild mint growing by the lake while Horace mixed bread dough to cook in his clay oven.

"When will the bread be ready?" Ysabel dropped a handful of mint leaves into a bowl of hot water. "I'm hungry."

"Soon, young Ysabel." The giant smiled down at her as he pulled a string of dark-fleshed sausages from his satchel.

Daniel and Ysabel looked at each other. "What meat do you use in your sausages?" Daniel asked.

"Pork, of course. I add onion, garlic, sage, and thyme for flavor," Horace said, ticking off the ingredients on his fingers.

They ate their meal of bread and spiced meat and drank cups of hot mint tea under the night sky. Ysabel looked up at the stars. "I have never traveled this far from my home. It's strange to think that my sister Olenna may be looking at the same stars. My mother told me that every star is a person who died. See that little one over there? That's Emma, Olenna's baby who died this year before haymaking. And the two stars next to it are my mother and Olenna's husband, Robert."

"There is the hunter," Daniel said, tracing a line of stars with his finger. "See, he is aiming at those two big stars, the eyes of a king stag."

"We see these stars from our village," Horace said. "We call those lights the hunter, but we say the two stars are the heart of the boar."

Daniel looked up at Horace. "Our poets sing of the wars between humans and giants. Do your people remember it as we do?"

"The storywomen sometimes tell us about the battle," said the giant. "They say the king of the humans, a small and powerful man named Breykker, warred against our grandfathers and took our land and forests. After he killed our king, Breykker and his soldiers drove the giants and their families over the big mountain. The soldiers lit the mountain on fire as the giants left. The fire spread and trapped many giant men, women, and children. A few survived and built a village in the new land."

"King Breykker died a long time ago," said Daniel. "His son, King Jeramin sits on the throne. There are fields of wheat where once there were trees." He paused for a moment and asked, "Do giants talk of coming back and reclaiming Liridian?"

"No, we are happy on our land. We giants do not make war. Sometime we fight, but it is man to man, not village against village."

"The map on the wall in the castle shows giants eating King Jeramin's guards," Ysabel said. "Why do you eat humans?"

"I don't," said Horace. "But other giants love human flesh. They catch sailing men who venture into our woods when they put ashore for fresh water. Giants like sailor meat, they say the salt air adds flavor to the flesh."

His talk of eating humans made Ysabel feel sick. She drank a mouthful of mint tea to settle her stomach.

"How many villages are in the land of the giants?" Daniel said.

"Three. There are five families in my village and about the same in the others. We come together after spring planting to feast and dance and tell stories. Unmarried giants and giantesses will look for a mate if they cannot find someone in their own village."

Horace yawned, then they all yawned and one by one rolled up in their cloaks and lay down next to the fire. Ysabel slept across the cookfire, away from the men. A few clouds moved overhead, backlit with light from the rising moon.

Ysabel rolled onto her side and closed her eyes. She dreamt she was in her mother's kitchen, eating a bowl of bread pudding. She tasted sweet raisins in the pudding and bits of ground peppercorn that deliciously burned her tongue. She woke with a corner of her cloak in her mouth. Spitting out the wool, she sat up and groaned, her arm and shoulder sore from sleeping on the cold ground.

The sky was white with stars after the passage of the moon. Daniel and Horace still slept. Horace was snoring. A slight sound for such a big man, Ysabel thought. Like the buzzing of a bee in her mother's flower garden. She fell asleep again and woke at dawn.

Ysabel knelt by the cookfire and blew on the ashes until a coal burned red. She dropped a handful of dried leaves and twigs on the hot coal. After the tinder caught fire, she laid a piece of wood on the cookfire, pulled on her boots and walked far into the bushes to relieve herself. When she returned, Horace was placing his clay bell on the fire. Daniel sat next to him, coughing in the chilly morning air.

"I dreamt about bread pudding," Ysabel said.

"I will make you pudding with lemon sauce when we come to a market," said Horace.

Daniel stood and gazed at the lake. "The water is calm. We should try to sail across it before the birds wake and disturb the fish."

Horace passed around pieces of hot bread and cheese. He handed a small jar of wine to Ysabel. Was it a different jar, she wondered, or was it the same one, a magical jar that never emptied. She raised it to her lips and the scent of pears filled her nose.

After the meal they took off their boots, tossed them onto the raft and pushed it into the water. Daniel and Ysabel climbed onto the bound logs. Daniel sat at the back and motioned for Ysabel to sit next to him so their bodies would be counterweight to Horace. Water flowed over the top of the wood when the giant stepped aboard, but the raft stayed afloat.

Horace sat in front of the mast with his legs outstretched across the logs. He leaned over and scooped his big hand through the water to start the raft moving. The red sail soon filled with a morning breeze and pushed them across the water.

Ysabel pulled her cloak tightly around her shoulders and watched the dark shore recede. She thought about Olenna and hoped her sister and Blane slept under warm blankets. She prayed the queen had sent food to them while they were locked inside the tower room.

The last stars disappeared in the brightening sky. Blue water spread around them, hemmed along the edge with tall trees. A brown smudge in the distance showed the canyons of the Anthra.

"Look, the firebirds are back." Horace pointed to a cloud of green birds approaching the raft. The birds swept overhead, chirping loudly in the morning air.

"I wish I could catch one to take back to my sister," Ysabel said. "She loves pretty things."

The flock swerved in the air with a rustling sound and flew back. One bird darted closer to the raft. It breathed out and a spot of fire flamed on the sail. Horace beat the fire out with his hand. Another bird approached and Horace flicked it into the water as though it was a pesky fly. A fish with a long jaw rose up through the water, opened its mouth and swallowed the bird. Its jaw was lined with sharp little teeth that looked like the cutting edge of a wood saw. Other sawfish appeared, swimming beside the raft.

The birds gathered in the air while the raft moved away, then sped toward them, swarming the boat and spitting fire at the sail. Daniel yelled and jumped up in a flurry of fast-beating wings, stabbing at the frenzied bodies while Horace smothered the flames with his hands. Ysabel lay across the raft as it rocked back and forth, clinging to the rough logs as she tried to keep it from tipping over. Birds bloodied by Daniel's knife fell into the open jaws of the sawfish. The birds suddenly retreated, hovering out of reach. The sail was a smoking char. The raft slowed.

Water washed over the logs as Ysabel sat up. She cried out as the serrated blade of a sawfish pushed up between two logs, scraping the side of her leg. She banged the head of the fish with the heel of her boot until it slid down into the water.

Daniel untied his cloak and threw it over the burned sail, stepping on one edge to keep it open. Horace laid his knee on the other side of the cloak. The cloth filled with air and the raft began to move again. The flock flew at them, spewing gold flames. Horace bellowed as his beard caught fire. Daniel scooped up a handful of water and threw it in the giant's face to put out the flames. Ysabel beat the sawfish surging onto the raft, hungry for the blood streaming from her cut leg. She hit their bony heads again and again, until her arm ached and bits of their broken teeth littered the top of the logs and still the fish hurled themselves at the raft.

They fought their way across the lake, reaching the shore as the sun rose above the trees. The birds rolled away in a green cloud; the pale bodies of the sawfish slipped back into deeper water.

One of the fish was caught between the logs when they pushed the raft onto the sandy dirt. Daniel pulled it off. "Is this good eating?" he asked and tossed it to Horace.

The giant cut off the jaw and quickly skinned the fish, wincing at the burns on his hands. He sniffed the meat and said it smelled good.

While the fish was cooking, Daniel picked up the jaw of the sawfish and broke it apart. He wrapped the end of one piece with leather cording, making a sawblade. He handed the blade to Ysabel. "You don't have a knife," he said. "This may be of use to you. I looked at the bindings around the logs. Those teeth are sharp enough to cut through the leather."

The sawblade was longer and lighter than her thread scissors. Ysabel glanced at Horace who was blowing on his burnt fingers and cut off a few strips from the hem of her linen shift. The cloth parted like water under her new knife.

After they finished eating she knelt beside the giant, saying, "Let me bind your hands." She wrapped the linen cloth around his blistered fingers. Each of his fingers was the size of three of hers. "I wish I had sticklewort salve," she said. "My mother used it on our burns."

Horace held up his bandaged hands when she was finished. "You are very kind. It is rare for a human to help a giant."

Not when they like to eat us, Ysabel thought, but kept her words to herself.

❧ Nine ❧

Daniel led them into the canyons along a sandy path stamped with hoof prints. Ysabel looked at the goat path that continued up the canyon wall and then down at Horace's huge feet. She didn't want to walk behind him. He could stumble on the narrow path and fall backwards, squashing her. And if he fell and needed help, how could she and Daniel pull him up again?

As if reading her mind, Horace waved her forward. "I will walk last, young Ysabel. I'll catch you if you fall."

"Can you walk that path?" she asked, ashamed that he thought to protect her while she worried he would slow them down.

The giant's deep laugh boomed off the stone walls. "I will widen it with my big feet, Ysabel. The goats will pass four together after I have walked their trail."

The sun rose higher, filling the canyon with heat. Braided tracks of beetles and looped marks of sand snakes covered the softer dirt along the side of the trail. Ysabel scanned the tracks; fearing she would see a snake coiled in the dirt, ready to strike if she came near. The path was empty; all the small creatures that moved along it were hiding in dark places, away from the hot sunlight.

They climbed the steep wall without talking. Daniel paused every once in a while to rub his sore leg. Horace hummed a merry tune. Ysabel called a halt to rest near the top of the wall. Horace flipped open his satchel with his bandaged hands and held the bag toward her. "Reach inside, there are apples for our meal."

While they chewed their food, Ysabel looked back at the land they had traveled; at the blue lake that looked calm now without the sawfish and firebirds disturbing the water, back to the forest where she and Daniel met Horace, to the top of the snake mountain with the Empty Valley beyond. She had come a long way. She had escaped from an old enchantress and met a giant. She hoped Adele would be at the castle when she returned. Her friend would be sorry she had not come on the journey when Ysabel told her about traveling with Horace and battling the sawfish and the fire-breathing birds.

The sun was at midday when they reached the top. Below was a maze of steep, flat-topped canyons. The ground at the bottom of the canyons was threaded with rivers gleaming in sunlight.

Ysabel shaded her eyes with her hand and looked at the surrounding canyons. "Where is the Anthra's nest? How will we find her?"

"We could yell." Horace cupped his hands around his mouth and shouted. The sound echoed around the steep cliffs. He yelled again. Daniel and Ysabel cried out when a host of black birds rose in the sky, alerted by his booming voice. Daniel quickly pulled Ysabel off the trail. They ducked behind a large boulder. Horace stepped behind them and crouched down. They peered around the edge of the rock, staring at the great birds circling in the sky. The Anthras soon lost interest and drifted down into their unseen nests.

"They are so big," Horace said. "They could carry off a giant child."

Daniel turned to Ysabel. "Did you see the Anthra that stole Princess Lira?"

"I don't know, they all look the same." She stared at the maze of canyons. "There are so many of them, how are we going to find the one that took the baby?"

Daniel knelt beside her. "Think back, Ysabel. What made the bird attack you? Did she smell food or was Lira crying?"

Ysabel thought for a moment, remembering the day at the pond. She had been holding the sleeping child and the meal Madron laid out had been cold, so it wasn't the sound of a baby crying or the scent of cooked food that attracted the Anthra. What had caused her to swoop down and grab Ysabel?

"It was the bell," she said. "The Anthra appeared after the kitchen girl rang a bell to call us to dinner." She pointed to Daniel's belt pouch. "The snakehead sounded like a bell when you cut it off. Try it now, perhaps the Anthra we seek will show herself if she hears it ringing."

Daniel opened his pouch and pulled out the rounded head. The mouth and eyes were closed. He threw it into the air and it dropped without a sound onto the dirt path. Ysabel picked up the snakehead. The mouth opened and one of the fangs bit down and punctured her wrist. She screamed and pulled the head away. The tooth clung, tearing a bloody line in her skin. She threw down the head. It fell, clanging like a sheep's bell, bounced off the trail and came to a stop, wedged between two rocks.

"It bit me," she said, holding up her bleeding hand.

Daniel wiped off the blood with his shirt. He bent over to pick up the snakehead. "You've not been poisoned, Ysabel. The fangs are dry, there's no venom on them."

"Leave it," Ysabel said. "It's useless."

"Look," said Horace and pointed at a single Anthra flying upward in the middle of the maze. The huge bird hovered in the air, turning its head from side to side, as if searching for the bell. Ysabel held her breath, wondering if that was the Anthra that had grabbed her and taken the baby princess. The bird flapped its wings once and soared toward the far end of the canyons.

"That has to be her," Ysabel said.

Daniel nodded. "We have to find her nest before she returns."

"I see a mound of red rocks where she flew up in air," Horace said. "We'll go in that direction. I'll keep the rocks in sight."

Ysabel cut a strip of cloth from her shift to wrap her wounded wrist. She took the snakehead from Daniel and dropped it in her waistbag. She wanted to kick the head over the side of the cliff for hurting her, but it had called the Anthra and might be of use again.

They walked up a rise, bending into a strong wind blowing across the canyons. Ysabel held her injured wrist up against her chest. The bleeding had stopped, though the wound continued to throb.

At the crest, both sides of the path fell away leaving a narrow trail across the ridge. Ysabel stopped. The trail looked no wider than her two feet. She had climbed the high cliffs above her village without a thought, but there were handholds and footholds to help her ascent, not this sheer falling off on both sides. Eye of pig, it was a far drop! One blast from the wind would send her tumbling over the edge with nothing to stop her fall.

Daniel limped across the knife-edged ridge. Behind her, Horace waited, still humming a tune. Ysabel took a deep breath and forced herself to step onto the trail. She turned her foot on a loose rock and teetered, waving her arms; terrified she was going to fall. Horace placed a finger against her shoulder to steady her until she regained her balance.

She hung onto the giant's thick finger and stepped onto the trail. The wind came up and blew hard, pressing her skirt tight against her legs. At the end of Horace's reach, she took a couple of faltering steps, and grasped Daniel's outstretched hand. He led her off the ridge onto firmer ground. Horace bounded across in two steps. Ysabel shrugged off Daniel's hand, embarrassed that she had been afraid.

They continued walking toward the Anthra's nest, stopping to hide whenever a black bird flew out of the canyons or returned with a big fish or broken-necked goat in its talons. The birds flew low enough to see that some of them had purple feathers on their breasts; others were marked with blue.

"Why do they have different colored feathers?" Horace asked.

"Could be one color is for the males, the other for the females," Daniel said.

By late afternoon they had arrived at the red rocks. The rocks were heaped against a large cave, a bowshot's distance across a chasm to the mother Anthra's nest. Her nest was woven out of tree branches and set on the flat top of a rock spire rooted far below in the canyon floor.

"I see the top of two white eggs and something dark moving in the nest." Horace said.

"Lira has black hair, that might be her," exclaimed Ysabel.

Horace looked down at his friends. "The nest is far away. How will we reach it?"

"We need a rope and a hook to attach it to the nest." Daniel turned to Ysabel, "Horace and I will give you our shirts. Cut them into strips and we'll tie them together to make a rope."

"That may not be enough," she said. "I might need your hosen."

She reached into her waistbag for her scissors. The knot of the old woman's white hair jumped into her hand. She tried to pluck one hair loose and the others clung to it. She pulled the hairs and they stayed straight. She began to braid them and the braiding held. The hairs lengthened in her hands as she worked them into a thin white rope.

"Look, Daniel," she said, holding up the plaited rope. "This is the hair I took from the old woman in the Empty Valley. It's turning into a braid, like the one she wore when I first met her."

"How are you able to make a rope from a few hairs?" Daniel asked.

"I don't know, but the hairs came from the old woman's head. They must be enchanted."

"Why did you start braiding them?" he asked.

Ysabel shook her head. "The idea of braiding them just came to me." She walked inside the cave, found a rock near the front and sat down, plaiting the hair until the white rope spilled from her lap and coiled at her feet.

The canyons had filled with the gold light of sunset when they heard the rushing wind. The mother Anthra had returned.

"What is happening?" Ysabel asked.

Horace said, "The Anthra brought back a dead goat. I hear the baby crying. She must be hungry." He watched for a moment. "The bird is ripping off pieces of meat. She's bobbing her head up and down. I think she's feeding the baby as she would her own chicks."

Ysabel made a face as though she had tasted something bad. "I hope Princess Lira will not be sick from eating raw meat."

"Now the Anthra is eating the goat and the baby is no longer crying," said Horace. He opened his satchel with his bandaged hands and pulled out a several apples and a wheel of cheese. "Our food will be cold tonight. The Anthra would smell a fire."

"You'll have to feed me," Ysabel said. "My hands won't stop braiding this hair."

Daniel gave her chunks of cheese and apple while she worked. Horace sat at the mouth of the cave, watching the Anthra. Stars had appeared in the night sky when he whispered, "Come see this."

Ysabel walked over to the giant. Daniel followed her, catching the rope that flowed from her hands. They watched as the bird stood on the edge of her nest, unfolding her immense wings. Her long end feathers spread apart as she pulsed her wings back and forth, as if gathering strength from the light of the rising full moon.

It was the night of the harvest moon. Ysabel's hands moved faster as she whispered, "The eggs are hatching tomorrow. The Anthra will kill the princess to feed her young."

She groaned as she thought of the little baby with the grey eyes. Lira would die in terrible pain. They might find a bit of her black hair or a few small bones that had fallen from the nest to bring back to Queen Ceradona. Olenna would be lucky to be sent to the mines. The queen might have her killed as punishment for the death of the baby.

"Ysabel." Daniel put his arm around her shoulders and spoke in a low voice. "We have come this far. We won't stop until Princess Lira is safe in your arms."

She nodded and walked back to the rock. Ysabel worked throughout the night while Daniel and Horace quietly talked or slept, one snoring while the other watched the Anthra's nest. Her shoulders hurt and her fingers were sore. She finally stopped at dawn when the air turned ash-colored and the hair no longer grew in her hands. Ysabel knotted the end of the braid and dropped it on the mound of white rope on the ground. She stood and stretched her back, and walked to the mouth of the cave, rubbing her aching shoulders. The men were huddled in their cloaks, asleep. The Anthra slept facing the dimly lit horizon, her head nestled in her feathered breast.

"Wake up." Ysabel whispered. "I finished the rope."

Daniel yawned and pulled his cloak tighter around his shoulders.

Ysabel nudged his arm with her foot. "Don't go back to sleep. We have to figure out how to attach the rope to the Anthra's nest."

Daniel rubbed his eyes and looked at the nest. "I could shoot it across if I had a bow and an arrow."

Horace sat up with a huge yawn and squinted, assessing the distance to the Anthra's nest. He shrugged his heavy shoulders. "We could tie the rope to a rock. I think I can throw a rock that far."

Ysabel sat on the ground and scratched her snakebite while Daniel gathered rocks. The bite burned in her wrist. She scraped her nails harder across the skin until the wound bled. She wanted to claw her skin open and chase the itch to the bone.

Daniel dumped the rocks at her feet. He knelt beside them, and one at a time, tried to tie them to the braid. One by one, the rocks slipped from his knot at the end of the rope.

Ysabel reached inside her waistbag for her scissors, intending to cut a small strip of cloth from her shift and bind her wrist. She brushed against the bundle of linen that the goose woman had given her and the itch began to subside. Ysabel pulled out the linen. It fell open in her lap, revealing the grey river rock. The rock felt heavier in Ysabel's hand; the tip looked sharper than she remembered. The itch in her hand ceased when she touched the stone, as if being near it quenched the fire in her bones. Ysabel placed the stone on the knotted end of the braid. It settled into the hair like an egg in a down-filled nest. A drop of blood fell from her wrist onto the stone. The fuzzy white hairs tightened around the rock as if seeking her blood.

Daniel picked up the rock and hefted it in his hand. "This will do. We'll wait until the Anthra leaves, then Horace will throw the rock at her nest and cast a rope bridge across the chasm."

"What if she doesn't leave?" Ysabel said. "She has the rest of the goat. Perhaps she'll eat that today."

"It was a small goat," Horace said.

Ysabel gazed at the white hair heaped at her feet. She looked up a Horace and Daniel. "Who will walk across the rope?"

"I will," Daniel said. "Horace is too heavy. You should stay here and wait for me to come back with the baby."

"But you're lame."

Daniel rubbed his leg. "It doesn't hurt much."

Ysabel looked doubtful. "There is only one rope, how will you cross it?"

"I have seen men wrap their feet around a rope and pull themselves across a river," Horace said. "Can you do that?"

"I'll try," Daniel said.

The giant opened his satchel, brought out the two sleeves from his red shirt and handed them to Ysabel. "Tie these together for a sling to hold the baby when Daniel travels back from the nest."

He unwrapped the bandages from his fingers. "My hands feel better. I'll make a meal for us before the Anthra wakes." He pulled out cheese and sausages and a jar of wine. He shook the jar, set it down and drew out a second jar. He sighed. "Empty, all my wine is gone."

While Horace cut up the food, Daniel reached into the pile of plaited hair until he found the start of the braid. He wound it around the base of a rock standing outside the cave to anchor the end of the bridge.

They sat at the entrance, eating and watching the nest while the sky brightened to a pale lemon color. The Anthra suddenly lifted her head and they heard the baby crying. Ysabel clutched Daniel's arm. "She's going to kill the princess."

The bird leaned over the baby and ducked her head up and down. "I don't hear the baby screaming," said Horace. "I think the Anthra is feeding the child."

Sunlight shot over the top of the canyons. The Anthra stood and shook her wings. The light glowed on a patch of purple feathers on her breast. She stepped up on the edge of her nest, folded her wings and dropped headfirst; plunging downward until she spread her huge wings, caught a breeze and glided upward. She beat her wings and flew away from her nest.

❧ Ten ❧

Horace drew back his big arm and threw the rock toward the nest. The knob of hair hurtled across the chasm, reached the nest and wrapped around the bottom, yanking the rope taut. Daniel pulled on the rope to see if it was securely fastened.

"Look," Horace said. "The rock is still moving."

The pointed rock wove up through the interlaced branches like a needle pulling a thread and emerged at the top of the nest. It kept moving, dragging the rope behind it as it sped back toward the cave

"Watch out," Daniel yelled and pushed Ysabel out of the way. The rock reached the cave, looped the rope twice around the top of the standing stone and came to a stop. Ysabel stared at the two ropes. Together they were far longer than the one she had made, more proof that it was bewitched. She frowned. The old enchantress had tried to harm Daniel and Ysabel.

What if she had spelled her hair to break apart in the air while Daniel was crossing over to the nest?

Ysabel shook off her fears. She had no time to make another rope from their clothing; the hair rope would have to serve.

They slowly approached the bridge. Two lengths of braided hair spanned the distance between the cave and the nest. Ysabel touched the top rope. The white line swung in the wind, as delicate as spider's silk. It looked too fragile to hold any of them. The weight of one of their feet would tear the braiding apart.

Horace looked down at Daniel. "You should go, the Anthra might return soon."

Ysabel tied the sleeves in a sling around the old man's chest. She hugged him tight. He no longer was the lame old man sitting by the kitchen door; he was as courageous as King Jeramin's bravest hunter. Daniel stepped toward the bridge. Before his foot touched the rope, the braided hair whipped from one side to the other. He drew back his foot and the rope stopped. He extended his foot and the rope moved away from him.

"It won't let me step on it," he said.

"Let me try." Horace held his big foot over the bridge and it sagged below the edge of the cliff. "It does not want me, either."

The men looked at Ysabel. Horace was twisting his beard hairs; worry lines appeared on Daniel's forehead. She stepped toward the bridge and stumbled, kicking a fist-sized rock from the path. Ysabel's heart beat faster as she listened to the rock clatter against the canyon wall during its long drop to the ground. She would scream the whole way down if she fell.

She put out her foot. The bottom rope didn't move. She withdrew her foot and held it out again. The rope remained still; it wanted Ysabel.

"I took her hair, the old woman wants me to walk on the rope." Her lips jerked as she tried to smile at Daniel and Horace. The giant's mouth turned down as if he was going to cry.

Ysabel slipped her cloak from her shoulders. "Put the sling on me."

Daniel knotted the sleeves at her waist. He held her and kissed her cheek. She wanted to stand in the sunlight for a long time with her eyes closed and her head pressed against his warm chest, instead of crossing an abyss on two ropes woven from an old woman's hair.

She opened her eyes and pulled away from Daniel. She felt in her waistbag for her thread scissors, careful not to touch the snakehead at the bottom of her bag. She handed the scissors to Daniel. "Olenna knows these belong to me. If I don't come back, tell my sister I tried to save her."

Daniel shook his head. "You'll be out and back in no time."

Ysabel wanted to believe him, but she was the one who had to walk across the bridge. She glanced at the nest. What if the Anthra returned while she was in the nest? She would have to fight the huge bird with her sawblade. She looked at

Daniel's dagger, wondering if she should take it with her, but it was made of iron and heavy. She didn't want to add more weight to the bridge.

She turned to the ropes, wiped her sweaty hands on her skirt, placed one foot on the lower rope and grabbed the top braid. She took a step off the rocky cliff, gripping the rope and keeping her eyes on the distant nest and the black dot that was Lira's hair. She moved her hands and feet sideways along the ropes. Her heart was pounding so hard she felt it beat behind her eyes.

Daniel called her name. Ysabel carefully turned her head. The edge of the cliff was behind her, too far to reach if the ropes broke. "Bring back one of her eggs," he yelled. "Drop it if she returns. She'll fly after it if her chick is threatened."

"Good idea," Horace shouted.

Ysabel nodded, trying not to shake the ropes, and slowly faced the nest again. She inched her way across the open air. Halfway across the chasm a hot wind blew up and shook the ropes, swinging them wildly back and forth. She clung to the handhold, fighting to stay upright on the slippery ropes. The wind shoved her again and again, as if it wanted to fling her into the air and push her down until she hit the ground. She was breathless with fear, too terrified to scream.

She heard Horace's deep voice yelling, "...bel, keep going."

Ysabel gripped the ropes tighter and faced the wind. "No," she whispered, as it whipped her braid against her cheek. "No," she said as her skirt twined around her legs. Her eyes teared up from the wind. She yelled, "No," a final time and forced her feet to start moving. She slid bit by bit over the abyss, not stopping or looking down until her foot hit the side of the nest. Ysabel grabbed onto a branch on the side and hauled herself up and over the edge.

She collapsed inside the Anthra's deep nest. She took a long breath and pushed herself up to sitting. Chunks of curly wool were stuffed into the woven sides to keep out the wind. The floor of the big nest was covered with dried grasses mixed with moss and grey down. It felt as comfortable as a straw bed.

Across from her the baby was asleep, nestled between two large eggs on a pile of down. Each one looked twice as big as a goose egg. A much smaller egg, no bigger than a chicken egg had rolled off the down and was lodged against the side of the nest. The runt, thought Ysabel.

She stood and looked over the top of the nest. The rope bridge flailed back and forth in the wind. On the cliff edge, Daniel and Horace waved excitedly when they saw her. She raised her hand to them then knelt out of the wind and crawled over the flattened grass to Princess Lira. The little girl's face was red from the sun and her gown was ripped and dirty. Lira moved her lips when Ysabel gently lifted her up but did not wake.

Ysabel held her for a moment. "You're safe now," she murmured and kissed the baby's soft cheek. She tucked Lira into one side of the sling, picked up one of the big eggs and pushed it into the other side, shifting it until she felt balanced with the baby on one side and the egg on the other. She put her foot on the edge of the nest, ready to climb out, then turned and picked up the runt egg. She would throw it if the first one did not make the Anthra turn away. The small egg felt cold in her hand; maybe the chick was dead. She was careful not to touch the snakehead when she dropped the egg into her bag, afraid its mouth would fall open and somehow call the mother bird.

She climbed out of the nest and stepped onto the braided rope again, pushing against the wind that blew hard against her, trying to force her back into the nest. She crept along the ropes, keeping her eyes on the giant and the little man at his side. Her friends were smiling and holding their hands out to her, as though they were helping her across the chasm and would catch her if she fell.

The wind died down. She stopped to rest. As she leaned into the hair rope, the snakehead squeezed up, past the runt egg and out of her waistbag. Ysabel watched in horror as its jaw opened. It rang as it fell, the sound echoing off the canyon walls.

She took a few more steps. Horace and Daniel were waving at her to hurry. Her snakebite was itching again, harder and deeper. It felt like a hot coal burning in her bones. She scrubbed her hand against the hair rope, trying to scratch the itch. She heard the sound of the rushing wind and turned to look. At the far end of the canyons, a lone Anthra appeared. She was beating her long black wings and coming in fast.

Ysabel froze, unable to move as she stared at the bird that was growing bigger with each rise and fall of her wings.

"Drop the egg," Horace yelled.

She thrust the large egg from the sling into the air. Her hands and feet barely touched the ropes as she raced across the bridge with the baby bouncing at her side. Behind her, the Anthra gave a loud cry. Ysabel felt the tip of a feather knock against her head as the bird wheeled in the sky and flew after her egg.

The ropes were falling away under her feet as she ran, shredding into bits of hair that swirled down into the canyon. She screamed as her foot plunged into the open air, then Horace was grabbing her arm and pulling her onto the cliff.

She stood, breathing hard, as they watched the Anthra plummet toward the canyon floor. Down she flew, her talons grasping for the white egg that tumbled out of reach. Her egg smashed into the ground and the great bird followed, crashing into the canyon wall.

Daniel shouted, "The Anthra and her chick are dead." He shook his fist at the giant black bird that lay unmoving on the ground. The body of a baby bird lay near her, surrounded by broken eggshells.

Ysabel backed away from the cliff and sat in the dirt, her legs suddenly too weak to hold her. The throbbing in her snakebite had quieted. She unwrapped Lira who was awake and screaming, angry at being bumped around in the sling.

"Give me something for her to eat," she said to Horace.

The giant opened his satchel and pulled out an apple. Ysabel chewed a bite for Lira. The fruit was so sweet and juicy that she could not help gulping down the first mouthful. She chewed another piece and spit the softened fruit into the baby's mouth. Lira swallowed the chewed apple and opened her pink lips for more. Ysabel fed her until the little girl's eyes closed, opened, and slowly closed.

She smoothed the baby's gown. "You need a bath."

Horace knelt beside Ysabel. "I was afraid for you. The bird was reaching for you with her claws when you dropped her egg."

"I thought I was going to fall." Ysabel scratched the snakebite and shuddered as she remembered being alone in the air with the pushing wind and the ropes twisting under her hands and feet.

"Oh, no," Daniel cried.

"What is it?" said Horace.

"Come look, the Anthra is alive."

The huge bird was awake and rocking from side to side on the ground, moving faster and faster until she was able to hop up onto her clawed feet. She bent down and prodded her dead chick with her curved beak. The lifeless body rolled over. The Anthra eyed her chick for a moment, turned her head and looked up at the cliff. Ysabel moved behind Horace, afraid of the bird's gaze.

The Anthra shook her wings, grabbed the sides of a rock wall with her curved talons and began to climb, her long wings swaying from side to side as she moved up the canyon wall.

"It will take her a long time to climb out of the canyon," Daniel whispered.

Horace kept his booming voice low. "But she'll reach us quickly when she is out."

"We have to leave before she gets out." Daniel helped Ysabel tuck Lira back into the sling and set the pace, hurrying them away from the Anthra's nest. They walked quickly down the path without speaking as they listened for the sound of the Anthra's wings.

Lira woke, crying for food. "Keep going," Ysabel said. "I'll feed her when we're at the ridge." She stuck her finger in the baby's mouth to soothe her as Olenna had when Blane was little.

They reached the ridge and stopped, panting in the hot sunlight. Horace passed around apples. Ysabel leaned against a rock and pushed bits of chewed apple into the baby's mouth while Horace and Daniel searched the sky for Anthras. A herd of shaggy-haired goats jumped up the steep walls of a nearby canyon. The lead goat landed with all four hooves centered on a ledge that looked too small to hold a human foot.

"How can they climb like that?" Ysabel said. "I don't see a path or a foothold."

"They learn early or they fall." Daniel dropped his apple core on the ground. "Has the baby finished eating? We should be going."

Lira kicked her feet, cried and arched her back when Ysabel attempted to retie her in the sling.

"Give her to me," Horace said. "I'll carry her." He held the baby on his shoulder and patted her with his fingertip. Ysabel was happy to be free of the child. Her hand and arms ached from holding the baby. Even with the sling, Lira was as heavy as a sack of flour.

Ysabel stepped onto the narrow path without hesitation. She wouldn't fall. She had recovered the princess from the dreaded Anthra, which was harder than walking a few steps across the ridge. She envisioned her triumphant entrance into the castle as she walked. People would cheer as she appeared with the baby in her arms. She would hand the baby to the grateful queen who would release Olenna and Blane and reward Ysabel with a big bag of gold.

Ysabel stepped off the ridge onto wider ground. She would give half of the gold to Olenna and use the other half to pay for passage on a merchant ship. She would travel disguised as a boy from a wealthy family and hire a man, Daniel? to accompany her on a voyage across the seas.

Or should she travel as a wealthy young woman? She looked down at her wool skirt and imagined a silk dress swirling around her legs as she walked across the deck. She would be beautiful, but rich ladies sat in their cabins all day, probably sewing, and not running to the side of the ship when the sailors shouted land ho, or scampering up the ropes to the top of the mast, or wandering freely through strange markets. No, she would travel as a boy.

The sound of the wild wind shook Ysabel from her dreams. Horace looked behind them and said, "The Anthra is coming. I can see her."

"We have to hide," Daniel said. "We're trapped if we stay on open ground."

The rocks around them were small, not big enough to hide behind.

"I'll stay back," Horace said. "I'll grab her wings and hold her while you escape."

Ysabel shook her head. "She wants the baby. She won't stop until she has her back again."

"Why does she seek her?" Horace asked. "There's other food for her here."

Daniel said, "Perhaps she thinks the baby is one of her chicks."

The wind blew harder. "She's almost here," Ysabel said. "Stop talking and think of something."

"We'll have to fight her." Daniel pulled his knife from his belt. Horace nodded and lifted his axe.

Ysabel scratched her snakebite as she imagined the upcoming battle—the men stabbing the great bird as she beat at them with her wings and slashed them with her sharp claws. She opened her bag. Her snakebite stopped itching when she pulled out the last item the goose woman had given her, the piece of undyed linen. She shook out the cloth. The square of brownish linen was the color of the dirt on the path.

"This might hide us." Ysabel looked up at Horace. "You're tallest, drape it over your head."

Horace handed the baby to Daniel and placed the linen on the top of his head. The edge fell to his neck. "This will not save us," he said, his voice muffled by the cloth.

"Hold it up," Ysabel said. As Horace raised his hands, a cool breeze flowed up the ridge, lifting the linen until it floated above the giant's head.

Daniel and Ysabel huddled close to Horace under the sheltering cloth as the shadow of the Anthra passed over them. Three times the huge bird flew overhead, screeching with rage, unable to see her prey.

Ysabel looked down at Lira lying in Daniel's arms. The baby's eyes were wide open as she listened to the Anthra's call. She's not afraid, thought Ysabel. The bird had fed her and kept her warm at night. The sound of the mother Anthra's voice would be comforting to the baby.

The bird flew toward the goats that were running across the top of the cliff. She slammed into a young buck at the back of the herd, breaking its neck. She lifted it and flew back to her nest, carrying the dead animal in her claws. When she disappeared from view, the cloth fell in threads from Horace's head and vanished into the dirt.

They ran out of the canyon. The raft was pulled up on the sand where they had left it. A mass of green firebirds swooped low over the blue lake, hunting insects in the late afternoon.

"I don't want to cross the lake while the sun is up," Daniel said. "The birds will try to burn our sail again or an Anthra might appear and catch us on the water."

A wave rolled across the lake as if something big was moving underwater.

Horace said, "I do not want to sail over the lake at night."

"Where will we go?" Ysabel said. "We have three days to return the baby to Queen Ceradona."

The giant man pointed toward the mountains of the south. "I will take you through the land of my people. I'll enter my village at night and take my father's boat while my friends celebrate the harvest. We'll row down the river to Breykker's Torch."

He looked at Daniel and Ysabel. "The old storywomen said the river flows through a tunnel at the bottom of the Torch. The tunnel is too small to allow passage for a giant, but it will take you through the mountain and out into King Jeramin's forests."

"Will you have time to take us to your village and arrive at the Northfast Sea in time to see the gold light?" Daniel asked.

"Yes, if we hurry."

Ysabel looked at the giant man who was twisting hairs in his beard as he surveyed the land to the south. Would Horace protect them when he met his people, or would he betray them to please the giants who had shunned him?

She took a deep breath. Horace had fed them, offered to fight the Anthra, and saved her from falling from the rope bridge. She could trust him. He was her friend.

❧ Eleven ❧

Horace kept them close to the canyon walls, concealed within the shadows as they headed south toward the giants' lands. Lira slept in the sling, cradled against Ysabel's chest. They left the protection of the walls at sunset and hurried into a tall pine forest. Ysabel was hungry and tired from carrying the baby, but Horace would not let them stop until nightfall, when they were deep inside the trees and far from the canyons and the home of the giant birds.

Daniel fetched a pot of water from a stream and built a fire while Horace looked inside his satchel for food. Ysabel fed Lira and washed her in one of Horace's small pots. The baby's skin was red and sore after three days of wearing soiled cloths. She cried when the warm water touched her bottom.

Horace heated a few drops of honey in a cup of water and handed it to Ysabel. "The mothers in my village put this on their babies when they have a rash."

"Olenna used barley paste for Blane," Ysabel said. She dripped the honey water on Lira's raw skin, waited a moment and washed it off. She patted her dry with the edge of her cloak and tied on a clean band she had cut from the hem of her shift.

Daniel reached over and stroked Lira's wet hair. "What a story she could tell."

Horace sat across the fire slicing bread and sausage. "The babe is charmed," he said.

Ysabel dropped Lira's torn and dirty dress to soak in the pot of bath water and examined her own wounds. The snakebite had closed to a wavy red line on the side of her wrist. The cut on her leg from the sawfish had bled slightly during the long walk from the canyons. She rinsed off the dried blood with a handful of bath water.

"Ysabel," Daniel began. "Tell us how you knew the cloth from the goose woman would cover us or that the rock would become an arrowhead."

Ysabel stroked her snakebite. "This itches when I'm in danger, sometimes so bad that it feels as though my skin is on fire. It burned when the mother Anthra appeared while I was on the bridge. It also itches when I need something and stops when I touch an item that could be useful, like the rock and the cloth."

She glanced at Daniel. "It's odd that it helped me and also called the mother Anthra."

"Do you remember what the old goose woman said after you caught her bird?" he said. "She told you that snakes had their place and could help you or be a hindrance."

Ysabel nodded as she thought of the old woman who had given her the two gifts that at first seemed useless.

"Ysabel finds everything she needs, even if she doesn't know at the time she needs it." Daniel thought for a moment and said, "I think Ysabel is a magician."

Ysabel frowned at the title. "I'm not a magician." According to stories her mother told her, magicians were powerful old men who lived in faraway lands and wore long black capes covered with jeweled stars. They had a fire in their chests, burning where their hearts should be. They used this fire to conjure up a bolt of lightning to strike the enemies of their king. Magicians were richly rewarded, her mother said, but their magic fire eventually burned through them, until one day they fell down in a heap of ashes that not even a dog would sniff.

Ysabel did not want to have a fire burning in her chest and she didn't want to drop dead in a pile of ash.

"You would be called a summoner in my village," said Horace. "Summoner is the name we give to giants who find what other people need."

"There's a little man in the castle they call a finder," said Daniel. "People go to him when they've lost something." He laughed. "Sometimes he finds the wrong thing; an iron knife instead of a silver spoon or a wooden bracelet instead of a jeweled ring."

Ysabel glanced at the snakebite on her wrist. The old woman's hairs, the rock, and the cloth were gone, but she still had a sawblade that would cut anything and the scar that itched when danger or magic was near. Perhaps Horace was right and she was a summoner. Being a summoner didn't sound bad, not like a magician with a fiery heart.

She picked up a stick to stir Lira's dress and dropped it, startled when she felt movement in her waistbag, as though a mouse had crawled inside looking for food. She opened the bag and saw the runt egg of the Anthra rocking back and forth. Ysabel pulled out the egg and threw it away from her, toward the fire.

Horace picked it up. It looked as small as a sparrow's egg in his hand. The egg rocked harder until the top of the shell cracked. The yellow tip of a beak poked through the crack and pulled back. They heard cheeping inside the egg, a soft, piping sound.

Horace gently pried open the shell with his fingernail. A pink-skinned bird slipped out of the broken eggshell into his hand. The chick was the size of a young raven with bony, flesh-covered wings that were sprinkled with tiny white feathers. Its big eyes were sealed shut under a thin layer of skin. Horace picked a bit of shell from the wiggling head. At his touch, the baby bird opened its pale yellow beak, crying for food.

Ysabel put her arms around Lira. "It's alive," she said. "Stop it from crying, it'll bring the Anthra."

"It's hungry." Horace chewed a piece of sausage and spit the meat into the bird's beak. It swallowed and opened its beak again. Horace fed it until the baby Anthra closed its eyes and slept, nestled in the giant's hand.

"You have to kill it," Daniel said.

Horace pulled his hand away. "But it's a baby."

Ysabel looked closely at the sleeping bird. "It looks so helpless. I used to find baby birds that had fallen from their nests. My sister said I couldn't put them back into the nest because they would smell like me and the mother bird would push them out again and they would die. I wonder if the mother Anthra would abandon this chick if she smelled you on it."

"Even so," Daniel said. "We must kill it. The Anthra will come if she hears her chick."

Horace closed his hand slightly, protecting the little bird. "I cannot hurt her."

"Her?" Ysabel said.

Daniel took his knife from his belt. "Give her to me then. I'll take her into the woods if you shy from killing her."

"No," said the giant and Ysabel together.

"She's alone, like me," Horace said. "Do not ask me to kill her. I'll take care of her. She will stay with me after you return to your land."

Daniel and Ysabel were silent. Horace was right, thought Ysabel. She and Daniel would arrive at the castle in triumph, but King Jeramin and Queen Ceradona would not honor Horace as a friend or give him a bag of gold. Every human in the kingdom would see him as a monster, a beast to be hunted. Horace believed he could not return to his village empty handed. He would be alone with only the baby bird for company while he searched for his tree with the golden leaves.

Ysabel squeezed water from Lira's dress and hung it near the fire to dry. "Tend to her," she said. "But keep her away from the baby."

Horace nodded and gently stroked the sleeping bird. "I'll watch her. She will not harm you or Princess Lira."

"How far are we from your village?" Daniel asked.

"We'll reach my home tomorrow before the sun sets. I'll fetch my father's boat while my mother and the rest of the village are at the harvest feast."

"What do giants grow for harvest?" Ysabel asked.

"We grow wheat and barley for ale. Our ale is famous among the giants." He licked his lips. "I wish I had a jug of it now."

Dark clouds covered the sky when Ysabel woke the next morning. She changed Lira and held her while she and Daniel waited for Horace to pull his cooking bell off the fire. He opened the lid and broke the bread into four pieces. Ysabel and Daniel took one, Horace ate the other two. He chewed a small piece to feed to the baby Anthra. Her pink eyes were open and her body was covered with grey down.

"I will name her Soleigh," Horace said. "That was the name of my mother's sister who died when I was a boy. She was kind to me. She told me that someday I would grow into a great giant."

"You said you had a sweetheart," Ysabel said. "What is her name?"

"Solmay." Horace sighed and fed the bird another piece of bread. "Her father chased me from his door when I asked for her hand. He said he would not let his daughter marry a man as little and poor as me. My mother found a girl for me from another village, but I did not love her and would not take her to wife. That was another reason why my mother made me leave our home."

Daniel swallowed his bread. "Will you look for Solmay tonight?"

"I want to see her, but I won't have enough time to find her and fetch the boat."

Ysabel dipped a piece of bread into a cup of sweetened wine and fed the softened bread to Lira. The baby wrinkled her brow when she tasted the wine, then opened her mouth for more.

"You said your people grow wheat and barley," Ysabel said. "Do giants raise animals for food?"

"We raise pigs for meat." Horace hung his head and said quietly. "Most giants prefer human flesh." He raised his head and looked at Ysabel and Daniel. "But not me. You are my friends. I would not eat you even if I were starving."

Lira lay in Ysabel's arms, staring cross-eyed at her small fist. Ysabel tucked her cloak around the baby. "Man-eating giants, the Anthras, firebirds, and sawfish; this part of the world is dangerous." She thought about her life in the castle, laughing with Adele as they sat together in the embroidery room or relaxing in the sunlight with Olenna.

"I'll be happy when I am home again," she said.

"Home is not always safe," said Daniel. "My father died at sea during a storm. All we found of him was a piece of his boat that had washed ashore."

He stirred the fire. "When I was old enough, I joined King Griffin's army. I took an arrow in battle for him and saved his life. After my leg healed, the king gave me a place in his castle repairing leather armor. Six years ago he asked me to escort his daughter, Princess Ceradona, on her wedding journey to King Jeramin."

He laughed. "Ceradona was disappointed when she arrived at Liridian and saw that her new home was smaller than one of her father's hunting lodges. If King Jeramin had not been as handsome as his portrait, I believe she would have turned around and sailed home."

"Did you ever marry?" Ysabel asked.

"No. Like our friend Horace, I had a sweetheart, but my girl did not want to be the wife of a cripple. She married a stonecutter."

They broke camp and walked along a river and around fir trees so tall that their tops poked through the dark clouds. Birds in the trees were bigger than the starlings and larks that flew over the fields near Ysabel's village. Their songs were different: deeper and gruff sounding, not the high-pitched whistles and chirps that she was used to hearing. From time to time, Horace looked up at the trees for freshly broken branches.

In the late afternoon when the sky had begun to clear, he stopped and pointed to a deep impression in the muddy ground next to the river. They stared at a footmark that was twice the size of Horace's big foot.

Ysabel backed away. "Your people are near," she whispered. "Are you sure no one will see us?"

Horace cupped his ear with his hand. "Shh, I hear voices."

The sound of shouting came through the trees. "The harvest celebration has started," he said. "You're safe here. No giant will leave the village during the feasting or enter the woods at night."

He pointed to a large bush growing on the bank of the river. "Daniel, you and Ysabel wait there for me. Stay close to the river until I return with my father's boat."

Ysabel grabbed one of his fingers. "Horace, I fear you will not come back for us after you have seen your people."

"I will return. My girl cannot marry me and my mother is ashamed of me. There is no place for me in my village until I come back laden with gold."

The sun dropped behind the trees and the forest grew cold as they waited for Horace to return with the boat. Ysabel's snakebite ached from the cold. Lira became fretful. Daniel dangled a twig in front of the baby's face to distract her, but instead made her cry.

Ysabel put Lira to her shoulder and patted her on the back, annoyed by her screaming. Muck and mire, babies were a lot of work. "When will Horace come back?" she said. "I'm hungry."

Daniel held out his arms. "Give the baby to me. I'll walk with her for a bit while you take your rest." He strolled away, singing to Lira until his voice was lost under the sound of the river.

Ysabel lay under her cloak on the damp ground. Rocks in the dirt jabbed her hip and shoulder. She sat up and looked around until she spied a sunny patch of grass inside the trees. The clearing was close to the river. She could wait there for Horace to return. She walked toward the sunlight, waving off Daniel who yelled at her to come back. Ysabel curled up on her side in the soft grass, lulled by the warmth of the setting sun. She closed her eyes and floated in her dream, back to the moment Horace felled the first tree to make their raft.

The itching in her wrist awakened Ysabel. The ground was shaking. A huge shadow blocked the sun. A bush next to her was pulled up like a weed and a deep voice, deeper than Horace's, said, "I knew I smelled a human."

Ysabel looked up and up. She thought Horace was tall, but he was a child compared to the giant woman who towered above her. The woman bent over and smiled. Her big teeth looked like boulders jumbled together. Tiny gold rings dangled from a gold bracelet around her wrist. The rings clinked together as she grabbed Ysabel around her waist and lifted her up into the air. Two big brown eyes stared at her. Ysabel could see herself in the giantess' dark eyes, a small figure struggling to escape the woman's tight grip.

The giantess laughed, gusting hot onion breath over Ysabel, tearing her cloak from her shoulders. "You are a little thing," she said. "But you will make a delicious meat pie." She laughed again, opened a long waistbag and held Ysabel over the black hole.

Ysabel twisted inside the woman's hand until she saw Daniel standing behind a tree near the river. He was holding Lira against his shoulder and staring up at her. She opened her mouth to yell at him to help her. The giantess let go and she was falling into a warm darkness that smelled of onions and dirt. She hit the bottom and was tossed from side to side as the giantess walked through the forest with the waistbag banging against her leg.

Ysabel grabbed a seam along the side of the bag and held on to it. She pulled out her sawblade. The sharp teeth easily sliced through the wool. She carved a small hole in the bag, put her eye to it and stared at the ground far below, a brown blur under the woman's enormous booted feet.

The path widened to a rock-strewn road. The giantess strode through a massive log gate and was greeted by several deep voices. She stopped and Ysabel saw the edge of a woman's dress, bright yellow and embroidered with red thread, and a pair of wool-clad legs that ended in boots made of green leather.

"I caught a human girl in the woods," said the giantess. She patted her waistbag, knocking Ysabel from her eyehole. "I have a tasty dish planned for the feast tonight." Ysabel hung tightly to the seam, trembling at the sound of the giants' laughter, knowing her cooked flesh was the promised fare.

While the giantess talked with her friends, Ysabel crawled back to the hole and looked out at the village. She saw an open area that was many times bigger than the village square at home. Wooden trestle tables, each one large enough to hold all of King Jeramin's court were placed in rows down the center of the square. As Ysabel watched, two giant men walked out of a cottage, carrying a long bench between them. At the far end, a giantess tossed a tree on a pile of wood for the harvest bonfire.

Surrounding the central square were homes of the giants, tall buildings built from tree trunks laid sideways, one on top of another. Thick layers of down-sloping pine branches covered the top of the dwellings. Flower gardens fronted many of the cottages. The flowers were familiar to Ysabel, but bigger than the ones that grew in her mother's garden. The black faces of sunflowers were as large as meat platters. Red and white hollyhocks grew twice as tall as the flowers tended by her mother.

Ysabel gripped her sawblade and thought of cutting around the eyehole until it was big enough for her to slip through and drop to the ground. She hesitated. She might break her leg when she landed on the rocky dirt or one of the giants might stomp on her to keep her from running away.

The giantess laughed again, shaking the bag. Ysabel grasped the seam, keeping her eye to the hole as the woman walked away from her friends toward the cottages facing the square. She stopped in front of a door that was made of wide planks of polished wood and latched with a length of knotted rope that looked thick and strong enough to tie up a ship at anchor.

Inside the kitchen, the giantess took a huge bowl from a shelf and set it in the middle of an enormous table. She untied her waistbag and dumped Ysabel into the bowl.

"Your flesh is sweeter than a man's," she said. "I need fresh herbs to bring out the flavor." The rings on her bracelet jangled as she rubbed her hands together. "Oh, everyone will want a piece of my meat pie tonight!" She picked up a long knife from the table, winked at Ysabel and walked away.

Ysabel heard a door to the back of the kitchen open and close. She scrambled to her feet, jumped and grabbed the edge of the bowl, pulling herself up until she could see over the rim.

Across the room, a three-legged pot, big enough for Ysabel to bathe in stood over a smoking cookfire. A shelf below a shuttered window held a clay jar filled with orange and yellow flowers. The flowers were huge compared to the summer marigolds her mother steeped in a tea as a remedy for headaches.

Ysabel dug the toes of her boots into the side of the bowl, trying to push herself over the edge. The worn sides were so smooth that she lost her footing and slipped down to the bottom. She tried again, and again she slid down. She shoved the side of the bowl in an effort to tip it over. The big bowl was too heavy and didn't budge, no matter how hard she pushed against it. She finally huddled at the bottom of the bowl with her head pressed against her knees, trying not to cry as she prayed please, please, please for Horace to have returned to the river and that he and Daniel were on their way to the village to save her from being baked into a pie.

The giantess returned, carrying a bucket of water and a fistful of greens. She laid the herbs and her knife on the table. Ysabel heard water being poured into the pot on the hearth. The kitchen soon filled with steam. The big woman pushed open the shutter and cool air flowed into the room. Ysabel could see dark blue sky and a sprinkle of stars. Night was coming on.

The sound of drumming came through the window. The woman lit a candle and worked at the table next to the bowl, humming as she chopped the greens to the drumbeat. She gathered a handful of greens and stepped away. Ysabel heard toward the giantess drop them into the hot water. She came back and stood over the bowl with her upraised knife. Candlelight flashed along the long blade. Ysabel tightened her body, trying to shrink and disappear as the giantess bent over the bowl.

The woman laughed and poked at Ysabel with her huge finger. "Now, now. Do not fret, little one. I will be quick."

Ysabel pulled out her sawblade and swung it upward, slashing the woman's finger. The giantess yelled and snatched back her hand. She glared at Ysabel and raised her knife again.

Ysabel ducked her head and closed her eyes, waiting for the blade to fall.

❧ Twelve ❧

"Hello, mother," said a deep voice.

Ysabel opened her eyes. She knew that voice. She leapt up the side of the bowl and looked over the edge, wanting to weep when she saw her friend, dear kind gentle Horace, standing in the doorway.

The giantess frowned and pointed her knife at her son. "So, you have returned. What do you want?"

"I missed you." The giant man smiled at his mother and winked at Ysabel.

"I told you to stay away, you are not welcome in my house."

"I don't have gold, but I brought you something else." Horace moved his leg to reveal Daniel hiding behind him on the doorstep.

"Man meat!" yelled the giantess. She thrust her son aside and ran after Daniel who bolted from the doorstep into the yard.

Horace helped Ysabel out of the bowl. They stood together in the doorway, watching the giant woman lumber after Daniel in the twilight, one stride to his three quick steps as she chased him through a grove of red apple trees and around a big pile of firewood. Daniel sprinted through a half open door into a large shed. The giantess wrenched the door open and followed him inside.

Ysabel looked up at Horace. "What can we do? I'm afraid she'll catch Daniel."

"Do not worry, Ysabel, he's small and fast. He will get away from my mother and meet us at the river. Now come, we must leave now before she comes back to the kitchen to look for you."

"Where is Lira?" she asked.

"She is wrapped in your cloak and well hidden. Soleigh guards her."

Ysabel ran to keep up with Horace as he walked away from the cottage. The giantess was banging around inside the shed, calling for the little man to come out, come out. Ysabel hated to leave Daniel. She had to trust that he could outrun the giant woman.

They were hurrying along a rutted path behind the village when they heard men laughing. They stopped on a dirt lane between two cottages to listen. A group of giants stood before the burning bonfire, drinking from cups as big as buckets. One man wore a heavy gold chain strung with three gold leaves around his neck.

"That is Grendon, Solmay's father," Horace muttered. "He wears the chain of gold leaves his father took from the king of the giants who was slain by King Breykker's spear. His father became chieftain of the giants who survived the journey over Breykker's Torch. The chain passed to Grendon after he died."

Several giantesses worked near the bonfire, laying platters piled with smoking meat on one of the long tables. Ysabel wondered if the meat was from pigs or humans. A group of young children, each child taller than a human man, chased each other around the edge of the square. Ysabel hid behind Horace's knee as he walked on, afraid the giant children would look over. She waited for a shout that they had seen her. She was afraid they would catch her and toss her about like a straw doll or pull her arms and legs until she was ripped apart.

She walked quickly with Horace through the woods. At the river, Horace reached up into a tree and untied the sleeping baby, wrapped snugly in Ysabel's blue cloak. Soleigh followed, flailing her bony wings as she dropped from the branch onto the giant's shoulder.

Horace pointed to a long boat in the river, moored close to shore. "We'll wait for Daniel in the boat and be ready to leave as soon as he appears."

Lira woke and sat cradled in Horace's hand while she ate a meal of chewed apple and sausage, kicking her feet at Soleigh who cawed when Horace tossed her pieces of sausage.

"I wish Daniel would come." Ysabel was cold and anxious to leave. "We have a long way to travel before tomorrow night when I have to deliver Lira to the queen."

"I'll go back and look for him."

Ysabel grabbed the giant's sleeve. "No, don't leave me alone."

Both of the babies were asleep and Ysabel was staring into the shadowed woods when she heard Daniel calling for Horace. "We're over here," she yelled.

The old man ran from the trees to the river. His face was white against the dark trees. Horace handed the sleeping baby princess to Ysabel and grabbed the rope line to steady the boat as Daniel splashed through the water toward them. "How did you escape my mother?" he asked when Daniel climbed into the boat.

"I hid behind a barrel and slipped out of the shed when she left to fetch a torch." Daniel wiped his forehead. "I felt like a rat being chased by very big dog. Ah, Ysabel, I am happy you got away."

Ysabel looked at the old man while he emptied his boots of river water, wondering if she would have urged Horace to leave in the boat if Daniel had not appeared when he did. She pictured the long knife shining in the giant woman's hand and thought she would have tried to rescue Daniel if the giantess had captured him.

Horace pushed the boat away from the shore. "The current is strong and the water is high. We'll travel all night and reach the tunnel through Breykker's Torch tomorrow morning."

They were far from Horace's village when the full moon appeared above the trees. Moonlight silvered the treetops and floated on the black water like cups of light. At Daniel's insistence, Ysabel spread his cloak on the bottom of the boat. She lay down on it, wrapped in her cloak with Lira in her arms. She closed her eyes, feeling the water rushing under the boat.

The two men sat on a board toward the front of the boat with their backs to Ysabel. "Where will you go after we return to the castle?" Daniel said. "Are you still determined to find the golden tree?"

"Oh, yes. I saw Solmay today. She was fetching water from the well and she was so happy to see me that she dropped her bucket. I told her I had to leave again, but I would be back soon with a big bag of gold so we could marry. Her father wants her to wed a wealthy giant from another village. He gave her until the next full moon to accept. That's enough time for me to find the golden tree and come back laden with gold."

Cold water splashed over the side of the boat as Horace paddled faster and faster, excited about his plan. "My girl is so beautiful, Daniel. Every man in the village wants her, but she is waiting for me."

At the bottom of the boat, Ysabel nuzzled the baby's soft cheek, astonished that a giantess could be thought beautiful.

"Come with me, Daniel," Horace said. "You could gather enough gold to live out your life in comfort."

"My friend, I wish I could. I find I am not eager to return to my bench, but I must take Ysabel back to the castle."

"But after, will you come to the White Woods? I'll wait for you."

"I am sorry, Horace, but I am bound to the castle and my king."

The river turned rough at dawn, slapping grey water against the sides of the boat. Ysabel woke at the sound of Horace's voice. Her back was stiff from sleeping against the cold wood. She sat up, patting Lira who was crying for her morning meal. Daniel had slept leaning against the giant. He sat up, his shoulders still covered with a corner of Horace's cloak.

An island of jagged white rocks reared up before them in the dim morning light, splitting the turbulent river in two. Beyond the rocks rose the massive bulk of Breykker's Torch.

"The river turns to the sea at the left of the white rocks," Horace said. "The other way takes you through the tunnel. You'll be on King Jeramin's lands when you come out of the mountain."

He and Daniel leaned into the paddles, cutting across the foaming water until they swung around the white rocks into a narrower and deeper channel of the river. The current was faster. The boat bounced over swirling water, moving past steep banks slick with mud.

"The river is rougher than I remembered," Horace said. "I should get out now." He stuck his paddle in the water, trying to slow the boat and turn it toward the bank, but the boat merely spun around and was carried sideways down the river. The men used the flat sides of their paddles to straighten it. They rowed the boat toward the bank. The strong current pushed them out again into the middle of the river.

Daniel yelled over the crashing water. "We can't get close enough to the riverbank to stop. Can you jump from the boat and swim to shore?"

Horace shook his head. "No, the water is too deep and fast. I would drown."

Daniel pointed to the mountain. "Then you have to come with us."

Ysabel clutched Lira at the sight of a black hole at the base of the mountain. The baby cried and kicked her feet against Ysabel's stomach as the boat gathered speed. Water smashed and foamed into the opening as if the mountain was swallowing the river.

Soleigh hopped toward Lira when the baby started screaming. Horace grabbed the bird.

"Watch your head," Daniel cried. Ysabel gripped the back of Horace's shirt, pulling hard until he fell back and they were sucked inside Breykker's Torch.

⟡ Thirteen ⟡

They careened into darkness. The last of the daylight gleamed on water-soaked walls as the river dragged them into the mountain.

Ysabel ducked when the top of the tunnel pressed close to the boat. Lira squirmed in her lap, unhappy at being jolted, her cries barely heard over the churning water. Soleigh stood on Horace's chest, beating her wings against the giant's hand as he tried to calm the baby bird.

The boat shot around a bend and the light was gone. It was so dark inside the tunnel that Ysabel could not see the others in the boat. Her heavy cloak was sodden with cold water. The front of the boat scraped against a wall. She hunched over, afraid a low hanging rock in the ceiling would hit her head or the boat would smash against the wall and they would be thrown into the black water.

The back of the boat swung about, banging them against one side of the tunnel and the other. Ysabel screamed and held tighter to Lira. Daniel shouted her name. His voice echoed off the rock walls. Ysabel yelled that she and the baby were unhurt.

Air in the tunnel grew colder as they were carried deeper into the mountain. Water dropped like winter rain from the top of the passageway, soaking their heads. The boat smacked into a large rock. Lira shrieked as Ysabel was knocked from her seat. Horace spoke in his deep voice, telling Ysabel to give the child to him. She placed the crying baby in Horace's hand and felt her being drawn away. She hoped Lira would be safer in the giant's arms.

Ysabel saw flashes of light at the corner of her eyes, but there was nothing to see when she turned to look. She felt the bow grind against rock as they whipped around another corner. She was shivering and her back hurt from bending over to avoid low hanging rocks. There was no light to see how far they had gone or how far they had to go. It felt to Ysabel as though they had been traveling through the tunnel for a long time. She wondered when they would reach the end of the tunnel, or, and this thought scared her so much that she stopped breathing for a moment, if they were trapped inside the tunnel, forced to turn and turn under the mountain until they starved to death or the boat crashed against a wall hard enough to break apart. She covered her face with her hands, whimpering as she imagined all of them flung into the swirling water, struggling against the strong current until they were pulled under and drowned.

She felt Daniel's hand on her shoulder. He leaned forward to speak over the sound of the splashing water. "Don't worry, Ysabel. We'll be out soon."

What if they could not get out? Olenna would be put on board a ship and taken to the faraway mines and never know what had become of her sister. And what about Blane? Ysabel thought of her young nephew trying to break rocks with a hammer too big and heavy for his small hands.

She saw a flicker of light ahead on the tunnel wall. Before she could call out to Daniel and Horace, the boat rushed forward and swerved into the light. The prow lifted high as the boat surged over a rise in the tunnel floor and they slid inside a huge cavern. The boat slowed to a glide. Horace sat up, blinking, with Lira and Soleigh tucked into the crook of his arm. The bird hopped onto the edge of the boat and looked around the cavern with her dark pink eyes. To Ysabel's surprise, Lira was asleep.

Shafts of daylight fell through cracks in the high ceiling, lighting a lake of milky blue water edged with brown mud. The cavern felt warm in the sunlight. Ysabel squinted her eyes, adjusting to the light and looked around the underground room. Layers of brown and white rock curved and bulged along the high walls. A flurry of white crystals, like a spray of frozen rain, shot from one edge of the ceiling. At the water line, the rock was streaked green where moss had taken hold.

They drifted for a few moments, gazing around the softly lit cavern. Small snow-white fish with large black eyes moved toward the boat, bumping against it before they darted away.

Daniel pointed to one end of the lake. Ysabel and Horace saw a heap of ivory-colored sticks at the back of the cavern and a long stick poking out of the water. Horace rowed the boat over with one push of the paddle, stopping beside the stick. It was knobbed at the top and looked familiar. Horace leaned over and gently touched it, stirring the mud around the bone. Daniel whispered to Ysabel that it was a leg bone and she understood that they were looking at the bones of a giant.

One of the white fish nudged the boat. Ysabel looked down into the water and saw the long bones of a hand lying on top of the mud. The giant hand was open; three of the outstretched fingers were intact, two were broken off. Ysabel cried out and grabbed the side of the boat. Horace dipped his paddle and the boat skimmed past the hand and a single curved bone as big as the rib of a butchered ox. He stopped next to a huge skull half sunk in the mud. The head stared upward through empty eye sockets. The mouth hung open, a toothless black hole.

Ysabel cried out and scrambled to the middle of the boat; afraid she would fall out and into the gaping mouth. "I want to leave." Her voice quavered. "I don't like it here."

Horace looked at the bones piled up against the back wall, the leg bone, and the spot in the water where the bony hand, the rib, and the empty skull lay in the mud. "These must be the bones from one of the old ones," he said. "The storywomen told us that one of grandfathers attempted to travel through the tunnel and return to our land to fight King Breykker. He was never seen again. He must have drowned inside the tunnel and his bones came to rest in this cavern. This is his bonepeace."

Daniel cleared his throat. "Ysabel is right, we need to leave or this will become our bonepeace." He aimed his paddle at rocks piled along one side of the cavern wall. "We'll look behind those rocks. There might be another way out of here."

Horace rowed the boat toward the wall. He hung onto the rocks with his big hands to let Ysabel and Daniel climb out of the boat and onto a rocky ledge. After Horace stepped from the boat, he sent it floating back across the water. "My father is dead," he said. "It is right that his boat stays here with the old one."

He led them along the ledge, past tall cracks that covered the rock face. None of the gaps were wide enough to allow any of them to pass through the wall.

Daniel put his hand inside a large crack. "I feel air flowing over my hand. There might be a way out behind this wall."

He and Horace put their shoulders against the stone wall and shoved. A few shards fell, not enough to widen the hole.

Horace hefted his big axe. "Stand back," he said.

Daniel and Ysabel, with Lira in her arms, moved away from Horace. The giant man swung the flat side of his axe at the crack in the wall. Ysabel covered Lira's ears as the cavern rang with the sound of the axe on stone. Horace's heavy blows shattered the rock, littering the ground with sharp fragments.

He stopped when he had made an opening wide enough for him to enter.

Daniel stepped through the jagged hole. He soon was out again and smiling. "There's a passageway with light in the distance. I felt a warm breeze; we must be close to the end of the mountain."

Ysabel held Lira and slipped through the hole behind Daniel. She waited as Horace turned to look at the bones of his old ones. He bowed his head for a moment, then sheathed his axe and squeezed through the opening in the wall, with Soleigh squawking on his shoulder.

They continued down a long, dimly lit tunnel. Horace walked bent over, his back just clearing the low ceiling.

Lira began to cry. "The baby is hungry," Ysabel said. "I have to feed her."

Horace rummaged inside his satchel. The big leather bag was almost flat, no longer filled with jars of wine and meat and cheese. He brought out a small round of bread and a few apples. The bread was days old; the skin of the apples was tough, the flesh dry. Ysabel chewed a bite of apple for Lira. Soleigh poked at a chunk of bread on the ground. She looked up at Horace and cawed.

"That's all I have, little one," said Horace. He rubbed his big belly. "I'm so hungry, I could eat a whole pig."

"I'll go hunting after we get out," Daniel said. "There should be plenty of rabbits in the forests outside the mountain."

Ysabel rearranged the baby in her arms and they began walking down the tunnel. The light became brighter as they turned a corner. The tunnel ended at a rock wall with a large blue circle in the middle. Tears filled Ysabel's eyes. The blue circle was the most beautiful thing she had ever seen, more beautiful than the painted glass window in King Jeramin's great hall. It was the sky outside the mountain.

"We're here," she said. She staggered a few steps, feeling light-headed. Daniel rushed to her side and took Lira from her arms. "This happens after a battle," he said. "We're strong when we have to fight and feel weak when the battle is over." He put his arm around Ysabel while she took a few deep breaths.

"I feel better," she said. "Let's get out of this mountain."

Horace was standing below the blue window. He raised his arm and grasped the bottom edge of the opening. "I'll lift you up," he said. "And then I'll climb out."

"You go first," Daniel said to Ysabel. "I'll bring the baby."

Horace leaned down and placed his hands close together. Ysabel stood in his cupped hands while he slowly lifted her up to the window. She crawled through the hole and onto a rock shelf. She had emerged high above the ground. A rocky slope led down the mountain into a forest of pine trees. She was startled to see that the sun was low, just clearing a distant, forested hill.

"It's still morning," she said when Daniel appeared in the opening with Lira squirming in his arms.

"I'm surprised," he said. "It felt as though we were in the mountain a long time." He passed the baby to Ysabel. "Put her somewhere safe. We may have to help Horace climb out."

She pushed Lira between two rocks to secure her. The baby waved her arms and screamed, not happy about being jammed between the rocks. Ysabel heard a thumping sound like boulder had fallen to the ground. Daniel was leaning over the edge of the rock window. "Horace fell," he said. "Watch out, he's going to throw Soleigh through the window."

They ducked as the bird shot out over their heads. Soleigh opened her wings, caught the air and flew cawing into the blue sky. She fluttered her bony wings, lost height and tumbled into a tree. She clung to a limb, wobbling back and forth as she tried to keep her balance.

Horace yelled that he would climb easier if he were barefoot. Daniel and Ysabel peered over the edge as he took off his boots and hung them around his neck. He pulled himself up, toeing the rough surface of the wall. When his head appeared, Daniel and Ysabel each grabbed one of his shoulders and helped haul him up. Ysabel felt as if her arms were being pulled from her body as she and Daniel strained to hold the giant's weight.

Horace heaved himself through the opening. He sat beside Ysabel and looked at the countryside spread out before them. "Are we in the old king's lands?" he asked. Daniel and Ysabel nodded, unable to speak as they caught their breath.

Daniel pointed at the tree-topped hill before them. "We're almost home; beyond that hill are the castle and villages of Liridian."

"I hear water running. There's a stream nearby." Ysabel looked down at her stained blouse. "I want to bathe Lira and freshen our clothing before we appear before the queen."

Daniel nodded. "We can make a short stop to bathe and eat and be home by late afternoon."

"I have a handful of flour left," said Horace. "If Daniel catches a rabbit, I'll make bread and stew to eat."

The thought of food made them rise. Ysabel tied Lira into the sling and followed Horace and Daniel down the slope. When they were on the ground, Soleigh jumped from the tree onto Horace's shoulder. He smoothed her wings, telling her what a fine bird she was.

Horace whistled as they walked into the woods. The baby Anthra made a chipping sound when he whistled, as if she were clearing her throat.

By midday they had walked around the hill. Ysabel heard the sound of running water. She pointed to a clearing in the woods. "Let's stop here."

Daniel left to fetch firewood. Ysabel undressed Lira, changed her soiled bands and wrapped her in Olenna's blue cloak. She fed the baby a bite of the last of Horace's apples and laid her in the shade. She gathered the baby's dirty garments. "I'm going to the river," she said to Horace. "Watch over Lira."

The giant tossed a chunk of apple to Soleigh and looked down at Ysabel, saying, "The princess is under my protection."

Ysabel walked through the trees to the stream. Rocks bleached white from the sun lined the riverbed. A wide course of water flowed deep and green through the middle. She knelt on the rocks and swished Lira's dress and bands in a pool of cold water. She rubbed them clean against rocks until her fingers were numb and the snakebite on her wrist ached from the cold.

She draped the clothing over a bush to dry in the sun and started to pull off her blouse when Daniel emerged from the trees, carrying an armload of wood for the cookfire. He smiled at Ysabel as he turned to leave, and then dropped the firewood, drew his knife and threw it into a bush. Ysabel heard a high-pitched scream. Daniel reached inside the bush and lifted up a fat rabbit with his knife stuck in its neck. The beast kicked its back legs once when Daniel pulled out his knife. He waved the dead rabbit at Ysabel before he turned and walked toward their camp. After he was gone, Ysabel pulled off her blouse and skirt, leaving on her shift. She scrubbed off the dirt and hung her clean clothing on a branch to dry.

The air blew warm as Ysabel walked across the white rocks to the river. She unraveled her braided hair, shivering as she stepped into the cold water. Her feet sank in soft mud. She crouched behind a boulder, pulled off her shift, and scrubbed dirt from the linen with handfuls of wet sand. She spread the shift over the boulder to dry and waded into the river. She dove underwater and shot up again, gasping at the cold.

Ysabel paddled across the river to warm up. On her return, she held on to a rock sticking up in the middle of the water and floated on her back. Bits of cloud, like milkweed seeds, blew across the blue sky. No huge birds flew overhead and no giantess lurked in the bushes on the riverbank, waiting to grab Ysabel for her stewpot.

She swam over to the boulder and sat on the sand. She examined her wounds. The gash on her knee from the sawfish was covered with a soft scab; the snakebite was a curving white line. She thought it looked like a snake as she scratched the tender skin around the scar.

Ysabel slipped on her dry clothing. She gathered her damp skirt and Lira's dress and walked back to the camp. Horace was stirring a pot of rabbit stew. She hung her skirt and Lira's dress next to the fire to finish drying and sat on her blue cloak, combing her wet hair with her fingers. She smiled as she watched Daniel feed Lira the last bite of smashed apple. When the baby had finished eating, Daniel wiped her face with his shirtsleeve and laid her against his shoulder. He sang a song of a little mouse that ate the grain and ran away from the farmer's rake, gently patting her as he repeated the rake, the rake, the rake, until Lira burped. He handed the baby to Ysabel, who was laughing at him.

"I had sisters," he said.

Ysabel pulled the clean dress over Lira's head and laid her on her cloak. The little girl was quiet, watching leaves move overhead in the trees.

Ysabel opened her waistbag and brought out her needle and linen thread. She held out her hand to Daniel. "My scissors. I gave them to you to deliver to Olenna if I did not return from the Anthra's nest."

"Ah, yes." Daniel pulled the blades from his pouch. "I am relieved that I do not have to tell your sister that I failed to protect you," he said.

Ysabel looked at his dirty hands and face. "You should bathe before we meet the queen," she said.

"Ceradona will see only her child," Daniel said. "She won't notice me."

"You have time to clean yourself before the stew is cooked," Horace said, pointing his spoon toward the river.

"Oh, have it your way."

"Our friend has stopped limping," the giant said as Daniel walked from the camp. "He does not rub his leg anymore."

"He's stronger because he doesn't sit on his bench all day," Ysabel said.

Ysabel's bone needle flashed white in the sunlight as she quickly turned under the frayed hem of her skirt. She would be home soon. Olenna and Blane would be freed and her sister would resume her position as wet nurse to the baby. Blane would be Prince Rowen's good friend again and Ysabel would return to the sewing room. She jabbed her needle through the wool, pricking her finger as she thought of sitting in the closed room, this time without Adele, embroidering garments under the watchful eye of Lady Clara.

Horace lifted the clay bell from the fire. "Will Daniel be content to return to his bench?" he asked. "And you, young Ysabel, will you be happy to go home to your village? Is there a boy who will be gladdened at your return?"

"No," she said. "The only man who has asked for me was old and looking for his fourth wife."

The giant man smiled down at her. "You are a kind and brave girl. I think the boys will line up at your door after they hear your story."

Ysabel cut the thread and smoothed her skirt in her lap before she answered. "My friends talk of the boys they are pledged to marry and wonder if their first child will be a boy or a girl."

She glanced at Lira, asleep on the blue cloak. "I told my sister before Lira was taken that I wanted to travel on a ship across the Drandelon Sea. But now all I want is to be home again with my sister and her son."

Being home meant living inside the castle walls and sewing all day. Ysabel didn't like the work, but she knew she was fortunate. She might have been given the harder tasks of working in the hot, noisy kitchen or toiling in the laundry, washing huge piles of the dirty castle linens.

She looked at the giant. "But what about you, Horace? After you take us back to Liridian, will you have enough time to travel to the Northfast Sea?

"I'll travel fast; I'll find the island of the golden tree and return to my village before the next full moon." He laughed. "I will bring home so much gold that everyone in my village will respect me and Solmay's father will agree to let us marry. I'll build the biggest house in the village and live in it with my wife." He scratched his chin through his beard, smiling at the thought of his bright future.

Daniel returned from the river. His hair was wet and his face scrubbed clean. They ate Horace's warm bread and rabbit stew that he had seasoned with wild garlic and a shaved root that tasted of mushrooms. Horace fished out a piece of boiled rabbit from the pot and placed it on the ground in front of Soleigh. The bird grabbed the meat with her beak and swallowed it in one gulp.

Lira woke up at the smell of food. Ysabel mashed a piece of meat into a cup of broth and fed Lira.

"We should leave now if we want to be home before sunset," Daniel said.

Ysabel wet a corner of her shift and rubbed dried food off the baby's face. Lira turned her head back and forth, away from her hand. Ysabel looked at Daniel. "Will you carry her until we reach the castle? My arms are tired."

"Allow me," Horace said. "This is the last time I will hold this little one." He settled her in the crook of his arm. The baby Anthra fluttered around Horace's feet until he picked her up and set her on his shoulder.

◆ Fourteen ◆

By late afternoon, Daniel and Ysabel stood in the woods at the edge of a wheat field. The wheat had been harvested while they were gone. Groups of old women and children were bent over the stubble, gleaning stray bits of grain. In the fallow fields beyond, men leaned into their ox-drawn plows, turning over the dark earth for the first sowing of winter wheat.

Ysabel sat down on a fallen log and looked across the field at the castle. Windows in the upper floors shimmered gold in the sunlight. People and horses pulling wooden carts moved along the road toward the open castle gates.

Ysabel took a deep breath and let it out slowly. "I feel as though I've been away for a long time." She was tired and still had to walk across the field before she reached the castle, but she was home.

She turned to Horace waiting in the shelter of the trees, and held out her hands for Lira. The giant stepped forward and laid the baby in her arms. Ysabel pulled her fingers through Lira's tangled hair and rubbed at a smudge of dirt from her cheek. She wrapped her cloak around the baby, swaddling her for the walk across the fields.

"I cannot go with you," Horace said when Ysabel stood up. "I do not belong in the land of humans."

"Oh, Horace. You belong with us." She hugged the giant's massive leg, holding tight, not wanting to leave her friend.

He leaned over and gently touched the top of her head. "I will miss you, young Ysabel."

Daniel looked up at the giant. "I don't like to leave you, my friend. I know you don't like traveling alone."

Horace sighed. "I'll be lonely without you and Ysabel." He patted Soleigh's head. "She'll keep me company while I search for the golden tree."

He glanced down at his friends. "I wish I could bring you both a bag of leaves, but I have to hurry back to my village before Solmay is forced to marry another." He twirled his beard hairs. "Mayhap Soleigh could bring you the gold."

"I don't want gold," Ysabel said, hugging his leg harder. " I want to know that I'll see you again."

As Daniel and Ysabel walked onto the field, they heard a harsh cry and looked back. Soleigh was perched high on the giant's shoulder, calling to them. Horace stroked her wings to quiet her as he moved backward into the trees, until they no longer could see him or the baby Anthra.

Ysabel followed Daniel across the field, feeling sad at leaving Horace and at the same time, excited about appearing before Queen Ceradona with Princess Lira safe in her arms. The queen would embrace her, free Olenna and Blane, and give Ysabel a bag of gold. She hoped Adele hadn't left the castle yet. She would hear Ysabel's stories and be sorry she didn't ride away with her to rescue the princess.

As they approached the road leading to the castle, Ysabel said, "We didn't kill the mother Anthra. What will we tell the queen? And what about Soleigh? How do we tell the queen we let her live?"

Daniel thought for a moment. "Say nothing about Soleigh, she belongs to Horace."

Ysabel laughed. "He'll raise her on apples and rabbit stew. She'll be like him and never eat human flesh."

"We'll tell a simple story," Daniel said. "We vowed to recover the baby princess after hearing that the king was too far away to reach his daughter in time. An old woman in the Empty Valley enchanted us and stole the king's horses. We escaped from her and met a friendly giant named Tall Horace who helped us find the Anthra's nest and save Princess Lira. We'll say we saw the mother Anthra fly after her egg and crash into the canyon wall before we escaped.

"People will add their own details," he continued. "In two days time you won't recognize our journey when the poets speak of it in the great hall."

After a few minutes, Ysabel spoke again. "Daniel, is Horace's island of the golden tree a real place?"

"He believes it, but I think it's a child's tale." He shook his head. "I fear our friend will not find his heart's desire."

"What will happen to him if he doesn't find the tree?"

"He'll have to return home. He said giants live where they were born unless they marry into another village. If he doesn't marry Solmay, he'll have to find someone else. His mother won't allow him back if he doesn't."

They entered the gates in the company of a girl herding a litter of pink-eared pigs and a merchant leading a horse and cart laden with bolts of woolen cloth. Daniel greeted one of the guards and pulled him aside.

Ysabel opened her cloak to show the black-haired baby asleep in her arms. "I am Ysabel, sister to the wet nurse, Olenna. We have returned with Princess Lira who was taken away six days ago by the Anthra."

The guard looked closely at the baby's hair and dress. "Oh, this is good news. Queen Ceradona has been in a passion since the baby disappeared. She ordered the guards to search the countryside again and again for her child, and has stood on the battlements for five days, looking for the king's return."

He waved his hand, motioning Daniel and Ysabel across the courtyard toward the doors of the great hall. "King Jeramin was gored by a wild boar four days ago. He was unable to ride and sent his men to the canyons to rescue his daughter. A messenger rode back this morning with the news that they could not find the bird or her nest or any sign of the princess."

A blackened log smoked in the fireplace of the great room. The smell of roasted meat hung in the air. Two kitchen girls carried platters of bread crusts and bones from the long table toward the passageway leading into the kitchen. They stopped to stare at Ysabel holding the dark-haired baby.

"Keep to your work," the guard said and the girls scurried into the passageway. He led Daniel and Ysabel to the dais in the middle of the room, pointing to a white cradle draped in white silk that was placed next to the queen's chair. "Queen Ceradona dressed Princess Lira's cradle for three days of mourning. She believed the princess was dead after the king sent word he could not find her. She will be overjoyed to hear that her child has returned. Now, wait here, I will tell her that her daughter is safely home." The guard ran up the staircase, the soles of his boots slapping against the stone steps.

Lira woke and yawned. Her toothless smile made Ysabel smile. She smoothed the baby's soft hair. "I'll miss you, little one."

From the passageway, the pastry cook bustled into the room followed by the two girls. "Bless you, Daniel," she exclaimed. "We heard you brought back the princess. Let me see the little darling."

Ysabel wanted to hide the baby under her cloak, disturbed by the woman's loud voice and her big red hands reaching for Lira. The cook touched the baby's cheek and brushed at a stain on the little dress. She looked up and backed away when Lady Clara appeared at the top of the stairs.

The lady hurried down the steps and ran toward Daniel and Ysabel with her hands outstretched. "The princess has come home," she cried. She took Lira from Ysabel's arms, kissed the baby's cheek, and put her against her shoulder.

She looked at Ysabel. "Where have you been, my dear? I was very concerned when you disappeared." She leaned forward and pulled a leaf from Ysabel's hair. "You look as though you've been sleeping rough. You must tell me your story later; now I must take Princess Lira to the queen."

Ysabel's arms felt empty when Lady Clara took the baby from her arms. Tears pricked her eyes at the sight of Lira's dark little head bobbing above the lady's shoulder as she climbed the stairs to the queen's chambers.

At the top, a tall man dressed in black, John Cauldgate, the king's steward, bowed to Lady Clara and smiled slightly at the baby in her arms. The cook and her girls hastened to the kitchen as the tall man descended. The steward walked toward Daniel and Ysabel. He stopped before them and held a small leather purse to Daniel. "Queen Ceradona wishes to convey her gratitude," he said. "She offers this reward to you, leathermaker, for the safe return of her beloved daughter."

Coins chinked inside the purse that he dropped into Daniel's hand. "The queen authorized five gold coins, but one was held back in payment for the king's horses that were never returned."

"And what of my sister and her son?" Ysabel said. "She is the wet nurse, Olenna. The queen ordered them held in the tower room until we returned."

"The boy was sent home to his village. Prince Rowen asked it of his mother. Your sister remains in the tower, I will see that she is released."

He turned to Daniel. "The queen will receive you tonight to hear of your journey. She is anxious to know why you and not the king's men were able to rescue her child."

"I was not alone," Daniel said. "This girl accompanied me and shared every danger. She deserves the queen's recognition."

The steward looked kindly at Ysabel. "My child, I am father to three daughters who will berate me for not allowing them the opportunity to hear the story from your lips, but Queen Ceradona holds Olenna accountable for the abduction of her baby and will not let her stay as wet nurse. You and your sister must leave the castle immediately."

After he left the hall, Daniel opened the bag and poured four gold coins into his palm. "Two for you and two for me," he said, holding out his hand to Ysabel.

She picked up her coins. Only two? She had undertaken a dangerous journey to rescue the princess. She expected a big bag of gold, not two small coins.

Footsteps sounded at the top of the stairs. Olenna came into view, leaning on the arm of a young guard. She coughed as she walked down the steps. Her skin was pale and she looked older. She had lost her rosy glow. Ysabel ran to her sister and embraced her when she reached the bottom step. Olenna's dress hung on her. Ysabel wondered if she had eaten since the morning she was locked in the tower room.

"Oh, Ysabel," Olenna whispered. "I was so worried about you. I didn't know where you had gone."

"We found Princess Lira and brought her home to the queen." Ysabel pulled away to look at her sister. "I have bad news. We are commanded to quit the castle. The steward said the queen still blames you for Lira being taken by the Anthra and demands we leave tonight."

"I am ready to go home now. There is nothing here for me."

"Do you wish anything from your room?" asked the guard.

Olenna coughed and shook her head. "No, I want to go home."

The guard escorted them from the hall into the courtyard where the castle gates were being held open for the last visitor, the wool merchant who was departing with his horse and empty cart.

Daniel strode over to the merchant and spoke with him. He beckoned to Ysabel and Olenna. "I traded a leather hide for a ride to your village," he said. "The merchant will take you to your door."

As he walked toward the armory to fetch the hide, Ysabel untied her blue cloak and placed it over her sister's shoulders. The young guard handed Olenna into the cart and tucked the hem of the cloak around her feet.

Daniel returned with a hide of rough brown leather rolled under his arm. He handed the leather to the merchant and turned to Ysabel. She hugged him tightly and kissed his whiskery cheek, trying not to cry.

"I will not forget you or Horace or Soleigh," she whispered.

She climbed into the cart. The young guard watched as the cart pulled away. Olenna huddled close to Ysabel and would not look back at the castle.

Daniel waved at her. Ysabel lifted her hand in farewell.

◅ Fifteen ▻

The cart rolled through the countryside under the darkening sky. The trees were turning in the woods beyond the shorn fields. Ysabel saw flickers of red and yellow in the changing leaves. She shivered in the cold air. She had left during harvest time, when the warmth of the sun lingered on the fields, and returned to the first chilly breath of winter.

Olenna put her arm around her sister, holding her close inside her cloak. Her arm felt bony on Ysabel's shoulder. "I was so frightened, Ysabel. I heard guards talking in the hall this morning. They said Princess Lira was dead. When Philip unlocked the door tonight, I thought he was coming to put me on board a ship that would take me to the silver mines. Instead, he told me that you had returned with the baby and I was freed."

"I came back as fast as I could," Ysabel said. "Didn't Adele tell you I left to rescue the princess?"

"No one but Philip was allowed to speak to me. He said a lady in a blue cloak and the old leathermaker were seen riding toward Darkmaren Hill on the day of the abduction, but no knew who she was or where they were going. I asked him to find you, but he said you were gone from the castle. Your friend Adele left that same evening. I thought you were with her. I wished for it. I hoped you were safely away from the queen."

Olenna pulled the cloak tighter around them against the night air. "Philip took Blane to our village to be cared for by our neighbor the day after we were put into the tower room. He said Prince Rowen had insisted my son be sent home. I will pray for the prince, that he will be as good a king as he was a friend to my child."

"Is Philip the guard who brought you to the great hall?" Ysabel asked.

"Yes. He brought my food and a clean blanket for my bed. He is a good man. He told me not to give up hope."

Olenna sighed. "I believed Queen Ceradona was my friend and would treat me kindly. I thought she would remember how I sat with Lira day and night when the baby was sick, and the many times she visited me at night to talk about her father's kingdom. I had to bite my tongue to stay awake while she prattled on and on about her father's big castle and his silver mines, until I wanted to scream at her to go away so I could sleep."

Olenna stopped to cough. "I am relieved to be shut of that place. We'll be home in our cottage soon and live in peace again."

Ysabel smiled to herself, remembering her sister's enjoyment of the comforts of the castle and her disdain for the rougher life of the village.

The horse pulled the cart through a copse of trees and over a stone bridge arched above a slow-moving river. Starlight trembled on the surface of the dark water. The road turned, following the river toward the village.

"We're almost home." Olenna spoke to the merchant. "Stop here. We will walk the rest of the way." She turned to Ysabel. "If we arrive in this cart, everyone will know we're back and come over. I'm too tired to speak to anyone tonight. Let them visit us tomorrow."

They climbed down from the cart and thanked the merchant. He snapped the reins and continued down the road. A few dogs barked as the horse and cart passed through the village.

Olenna and Ysabel walked along the dirt road until they reached the first cottage on the edge of the village. The windows were dark. Hens in a coop set inside a fenced garden clucked sleepily as they walked past. Cottages with thatched roofs were clustered around the village square. Every door was closed, every window shuttered. Here and there a candle burned in an upper room, but no one looked out at their quiet footfalls.

Their mother's cottage faced the village well. A wattle fence to the side of the cottage bowed outward from the mass of dead flower stalks pushing against it. Behind the dried stalks, new mounds of dirt had been dug up and covered with straw.

"Our neighbor was quick to move into our mother's garden," Olenna murmured. She lifted the latch to the front door and they stepped into the kitchen that was dark and cold and smelled of mice.

Olenna crossed the room and opened the shutter over the kitchen counter, letting in fresh air and the gleam of starlight. A table and several stools were pushed against the wall. Cold firebricks surrounded the black hearth. A bundle of dried herbs hung from a peg above an empty shelf. At the end of the room, a patched linen curtain separated the kitchen and the sleeping room.

"I'll fetch Blane if you like," Ysabel said.

"No, if we wake him now, he'll be excited to see us and not go back to sleep."

Olenna knelt to pull a wooden chest from under the table and unlocked it with a key from her waistbag. She took out a teapot and two cups and handed them to Ysabel. She shook out a woolen blanket, scattering dried mint leaves she had packed with the blanket to repel moths, a linen sheet, and layers of their mother's heavy woolen clothing: a brown cloak, a long skirt, and a blouse. At the bottom of the chest lay a neatly folded red wool bodice, a green wool skirt, a linen shift, and a blouse of lightweight blue wool; their mother's finest clothing that she had worn to village festivals.

Olenna tossed the cloak onto a stool. "Use this until I can send someone to fetch your cloak from the castle." She looked at her sister. "I am sorry you had to leave. It was my fault."

"I was to blame," Ysabel said. "Princess Lira was taken by the Anthra when I was holding her sleeping basket."

"I shouldn't have slept while she was in my care," Olenna said. "But no matter, she's safe and we're home and together again."

She got to her feet. "We'll set up our house tomorrow, after we've had a sound night's sleep." She picked up the sheet and blanket and carried them through the curtain into the back room.

Ysabel set the teapot and cups on the counter. She was pushing a firebrick back into place with the toe of her boot when Olenna reentered the room.

"The roof didn't leak and the straw in our bed is musty but dry. We'll sleep on it tonight and stuff it new tomorrow." Olenna opened her waistbag and pulled out a small round of bread. "I saved this after I heard Queen Ceradona had started mourning her daughter. I feared every moment a guard would come and take me away. I didn't know when I would eat next."

They sat at the table in the dim starlight, eating bread while Ysabel recounted her travels. "After you were taken to the tower, I tried to find someone to help me save Princess Lira," she said. "First everyone said to leave it for the king and his men, then his men at the dining table said the king would not find the baby in time. They didn't even try, Olenna, they were more interested in eating their meat then searching for the princess, so I stole one of the king's horses to ride to the canyons where Madron said the Anthra had her nest. I wore your blue cloak because Adele said no one would stop me if I wore the queen's color. Daniel, the leathermaker, came after me. He wanted to take the horses back, but an old goose woman shamed him into coming with me through the Darkmaren Forest."

Olenna put her hand over her heart when Ysabel described escaping from the old woman in the Empty Valley, meeting a kindly giant named Horace, and fighting firebirds and sawfish as they sailed across the blue lake.

"I would be scared witless if I saw a giant." Olenna said.

"Horace is gentle and friendly. He doesn't eat humans, he liked us." Ysabel sighed. "I don't think I'll ever see him again. He is on a quest to find gold so he may return to his village a wealthy man and marry the girl he loves."

Ysabel continued her story, telling her sister about weaving the rope and her terrifying walk across the bridge to the Anthra's nest.

"How did you know you could use her hair to make the rope?" Olenna asked.

"I saw the hairs in her comb and felt I should take them. She took some of mine when she pulled a dried flower from my hair. I think she used my hair to turn hers red and become young again."

"She was an enchantress," Olenna said.

Ysabel showed Olenna the scar from her snakebite. "I got this before we met Horace. It itches when something I need is close at hand. I was looking for something to make a rope and the scar stopped itching when I touched the knot of the old woman's hair. I started braiding the hair and kept going until I made a long rope. I attached a rock the goose woman gave to me to the end of the rope. Horace threw it to the nest and it wrapped around twice and came back to us to make a bridge."

She added, "Daniel and Horace said I was a summoner because I could call magic from items like the rock and the old woman's hair."

Olenna gazed at her sister. "You turned three hairs into a long rope, mayhap you do have magical powers." She dropped the last bite of her bread in front of Ysabel. "Are you like the magicians our mother told us about? Can you cast a spell and conjure a whole round of bread from this crumb?"

Ysabel laughed. "It wasn't that kind of magic. I can't make something happen by wishing it. It's as though there was a power inside the object that appeared when I needed it." She shook her head. "I don't know if I have it anymore. I don't need anything to help me now that we're home."

"Except for food," Olenna said. "But we'll manage that." She yawned. "Tell me the rest of your story and then we'll go to bed."

Ysabel told her about stealing the egg that hatched into a baby Anthra, being captured by a giantess and rescued by Horace. When she was finished, Ysabel opened her waistbag and pulled out the sawblade. "Daniel made this for me after we crossed the lake. It's from a sawfish and can cut through anything." She spun it on the table. "I used this to cut a hole in the giantess's bag when she grabbed me. I stabbed her with it when she was going to chop me up." She looked at the slowing blade. "This and my scar are all I have to remember my journey."

Olenna gingerly touched one of the pointed teeth. "You speak calmly, Ysabel, but weren't you frightened when you faced the Anthra or when the giantess grabbed you?"

Ysabel traced the snakebite on her wrist while she considered Olenna's question. "I was scared but I had to save Princess Lira or the queen would have sent you and Blane to work in the silver mines."

She looked around the kitchen. "This is our home, but it feels strange to be here instead of sitting around a cookfire with Daniel and Horace and Lira and the baby Anthra. We were afraid of Soleigh at first; that's her name. We feared her mother would hear her cry and come after her. But she didn't call her mother once; she wanted to be with us." Ysabel wiped tears from her eyes. "I miss them, they're my friends."

"I would like to see Lira again," Olenna said. "She is a sweet baby. I hope the queen finds a good wet nurse for her."

"The mother Anthra fed her raw goat meat and she's eaten bread and rabbit and apple that I chewed for her," Ysabel said. "Queen Ceradona may find her baby no longer wants to suckle but is ready to eat meat from the bone."

Olenna laughed and reached over the table to squeeze Ysabel's hand. "You were brave, little sister. You saved the princess when the king and all of his men could not do so. Your story will be on everyone's lips tomorrow. You will be telling it from winter to spring."

"Our neighbors will ask why we left the castle and returned to the village," Ysabel said.

"They'll know soon enough of the queen's ill will toward me. But we're not alone, we aren't the only people who have had hard dealings with the castle."

Olenna twisted the sapphire ring that hung loose on her finger. "I'll sell my ring tomorrow for meat and flour to feed us through winter."

"I'll find nuts in the woods and gather eggs from the cliffs."

"That will help," said Olenna. "I'll keep money back from my ring to buy chickens and a pig in spring." She glanced around the cottage. "We have a lot of work to do before winter."

"We'll manage."

"We will, but it would be easier if there was a man in the house to help us."

""Is Philip sweet on you?" Ysabel said. "Will he visit you in the village?"

Olenna shrugged. "I don't know. He was kind to me but his life is in the castle. I may never see him again." She looked at her sister. "You'll soon be of an age to wed."

"I don't want to marry."

Olenna shook her head. "You have little choice, Ysabel. Your life is in the village now." She stretched her arms over her head and yawned again. "Now summon sleep, my dear. It's late and time we were in bed."

Ysabel opened the kitchen door after Olenna left and stood in the doorway, gazing at the sleeping village. The cottages around the square looked smaller than the shed behind the giantess's house. The entire village seemed smaller. She shifted from foot to foot, feeling restless. She sighed, her breath a white puff in the night air. Tomorrow she would clean the cottage with Olenna and take Blane into the woods to gather firewood and search for nuts. Ysabel sighed again. Her life in the village would be tame compared to traveling to the far ends of the land, outrunning the claws of the Anthra, and becoming good friends with a giant.

She shivered in the cold air and thought of Horace sleeping in the woods with the baby Anthra as his only company. She hoped he wasn't lonely. Ysabel slowly closed the door and the shutter and walked through the curtain into the sleeping room. She took off her skirt and blouse and hung them on a hook next to Olenna's dress. She smoothed the linen shift over her hips, pulled back the sheet and lay down beside her sister in the family bed.

⤙ Sixteen ⤚

Ysabel woke before dawn and rolled from the mattress, careful not to rustle the straw and wake her sister. She pulled on Olenna's old boots. They had stretched during the long journey and felt looser on her feet. She unhooked her skirt and blouse and her mother's heavy wool cloak from the wall, stopping as she left the room to press her face into Olenna's blue cloak and inhale the strong smell of wood smoke.

She dropped her clothing on a stool in the kitchen and opened the shutter and the door. She stood for a moment in her shift, breathing in the cold morning air. Ysabel took a straw broom leaning against a wall and swept dust and mouse droppings from the floor and out the door. When the floor was clean, she stripped a handful of dried sage from the bundled herbs hanging on the wall and dropped the leaves into the pot to make tea for Olenna's cough.

Ysabel placed the teapot and a cup on the table and sat on a stool, chewing the last bite of cold bread. She smiled, remembering Horace cooking dough in his clay oven in the morning while Soleigh hopped in front of him, impatient for a bite of warm bread.

The sky outside the window was grey with early light. Ysabel wondered if Daniel was awake. She wanted to talk with him and cling a little longer to their journey. She looked at the pile of her old clothes. The blouse still showed stains. The wool skirt was faded and too short after she had hemmed it to cover the ragged edge.

Ysabel lifted the lid to the wooden chest and pushed past her mother's winter skirt and blouse to the finer clothing underneath. She hesitated. The lightweight wools would be more comfortable to wear as the day grew warm, but she couldn't take them, their mother's best clothing rightly belonged to Olenna. But the good shift, ah, that she would take. She dressed in the long shift that fell above her ankles, the heavy skirt, and the overblouse. Coins clinked inside her bag as she tied it to her waist. "I forgot about you," she said and spilled the two gold coins into her hand. One side of each coin was stamped with crossed sheaves of wheat, the wealth of the kingdom. The other side showed King Jeramin with his long hair curling to his shoulders, holding a raised sword in his hand. Ysabel laid one of the coins on the table next to the teapot and slipped the other into her waistbag. She thrust her sawblade through the ties, pulled on her mother's cloak and stood in the doorway. She heard voices from the other cottages and the sound of a shuttered window being opened.

Ysabel closed the door behind her and walked around the wattle fence and down the sunken path to the river. Mist hung white and shaggy over the water, orange leaves in the woods dripped dew. A bird broke from a branch in front of her; drops of water spun behind it as it flew away.

Flocks of black crows circled overhead as she walked from the river and across a harvested field to the castle. A few clouds above the horizon were flushed pink from the light of the rising sun. Ysabel stopped walking, entranced by the beautiful light until the clouds faded to light grey and blew away in the morning breeze.

She arrived at the castle as two guards were pushing open the tall gates to admit a crowd of people carrying baskets and jars of goods for the castle. Inside the walls, housemaids chatted in the courtyard as they emptied buckets of white ash on the compost pile between the chicken coops and kennels for the scent dogs. A woman stood inside the fenced coops, scattering handfuls of feed to red-breasted chickens pecking busily at her feet. In the herber, two gardeners were cutting stems of lavender and rosemary to scent the floor of the queen's chambers. A young girl knelt on the path, filling a basket with mint leaves for the kitchen.

The door to the kitchen was propped open to let in the fresh morning air. Ysabel heard the cooks talking and the thwack of their knives on the chopping table. She wrapped her cloak around her and sat on Daniel's bench to wait for him.

She fell asleep and woke to his laughter as he stepped out of the kitchen. He held a large pastry in his hand and wore new boots of red-dyed leather.

Ysabel jumped up from the bench. "Did you tell our story to the queen?" she asked.

"Dear child," he smiled. "It is good to see you. Ah, I know what you want." Daniel handed the pastry to Ysabel. "Cook gave me an extra apple bunty. She thinks I did not eat once during the six days we were gone." He laughed. "My, you were hungry. Now come with me, I have something for you and your sister."

Ysabel started to wipe her hands on her mother's skirt. She licked her fingers instead as she walked beside Daniel toward the armory. She felt happy as she breathed in his familiar scent of leather and sweat.

Daniel opened the door to his workroom. Long wooden rods mounted on the wall held smooth-finished hides and leather straps cut in different widths. A worktable stood under an open window with two bags set on one end, next to a string of sausages and a round of bread.

"That's for you." Daniel pointed to the food. "There's flour and barley in the bags. Cook gave them to me after I told her I was worried that you and your sister were going home to empty cupboards."

"This is kind of you. My sister plans to sell a ring this morning to buy enough food to feed us through the winter, but she'll be grateful for a bite of fresh bread before she begins her day."

"How is your sister feeling? She was coughing last night."

"She's a little weak from her stay in the tower, but she'll recover quickly now that she's home."

Daniel took down a big leather bag from a hook. "I planned to ride to your cottage later today and take food to you but you could take it now if you like." He glanced at Ysabel. "If the bag is too heavy, you could take the bread and I'll bring the rest later."

Ysabel laughed. "I can manage. That bag is no heavier than Princess Lira and I carried her for most of three days."

While Daniel stuffed the food into the leather bag, Ysabel wandered over to the table. A leather case holding a row of bronze needles lay open on the table, next to a polishing stone, various knives, and a small bowl filled with iron buckles. She picked up a curved knife. "I came this morning because I missed you and Horace." She put down the knife. "I thought of him sleeping in the woods last night. I feared he was lonely because we weren't with him."

Daniel nodded. "Me too. I even missed his snoring, but Horace is far from Liridian by now, looking for his golden tree."

"I told my sister about our journey. She said everyone in our village would want to hear me tell my story. She said I'd be telling it through winter."

"And why not?" Daniel said. "It is a handsome tale. I entertained Queen Ceradona and her ladies last night with an account of our travels. I think they forgot to breathe when they heard of the brave girl who walked across an abyss on ropes woven from an old woman's hair to rescue Princess Lira from the nest of the monstrous Anthra. Their eyes were as big as goose eggs when I spoke of our friend, Tall Horace, who defied his giantess mother to save you from her stewpot."

He rubbed his throat. "I talked so long I had to drink a jug of ale to keep my tongue from drying up and falling out of my mouth."

"Did you tell them about the tunnel through Breykker's Torch and the lake of bones?"

"I did. I said we passed through the bonepeace of a giant who drowned inside the mountain when he attempted to return to Liridian." Daniel shook his head. "They smiled at that part. When I was done, they wanted to hear the whole story again. I am commanded to recite it to the king when he returns tomorrow to enliven his recovery."

He looked at Ysabel. "I would like you to be with me. I think the king and queen would enjoy hearing the tale from you, too."

"I do not want to appear before Queen Ceradona. She locked my sister in the tower for six days and turned us out last night after we brought back Princess Lira." Ysabel looked out of the window at the castle. "She should have begged Olenna's pardon for punishing her and given us a bigger reward. Muck and mire, was her daughter's life worth only four coins?"

"They were gold coins, Ysabel, not bronze," Daniel said. "The queen did not send us on our journey or promise a payment for her daughter's safe return. She believes she was generous to give us anything."

He joined Ysabel at the window. "Understand the queen's anger, my girl. She was afraid for her child and wanted to blame someone. Your sister was closest at hand."

He smiled at her. "I heard that not all wanted your sister gone from the castle. Cook says one of the guards is eager to see Olenna again."

"He'll have to meet her at our cottage. Olenna feels she was ill-used by the queen. She'll never return to the castle."

Two guards walked past the window. Ysabel recognized the tall man with a grey beard as the queen's guard who had taken Olenna to the tower room. The younger man with him had carried Blane.

"The giant sniffs around the castle," the young guard said. "A peasant found his footmark this morning in a muddy patch on the road. He said the mark was bigger than the feet of five men put together. I say we hunt him tomorrow before King Jeramin returns. A dead giant would be a grand gift to present to the king."

He grasped the hilt of his sword. Ysabel saw the look on his face, as if he had spied a fat buck and could not wait to draw an arrow on it.

"What say you?" he asked his fellow guard. "Do we bring back the whole giant or just his head?"

The greybeard laughed. "The head bones would look fine boiled and mounted in the great hall. But we wait for the king.

He returns tomorrow. After a good night's rest and he might feel able to lead the hunt."

Ysabel and Daniel looked at each other as the men walked toward the tall doors to the hall.

"Horace did not leave," Daniel said.

"Why does he stay?"

"I don't know. He said he was heading toward the Northfast Sea and yet he lingers." Daniel picked up his cloak from his worktable. It looked new and made of heavier wool. Ysabel thought they'd both be sweating in their winter clothing before midday. Daniel swung the cloak around his shoulders. "I'll look for him in the North Woods and ask what he needs. He's in danger if he tarries in this land."

"I'm coming with you."

"No, you go home and take care of your sister. I'll carry your greeting to our friend."

"Take the food with you," Ysabel said. "Horace doesn't have anything left in his satchel to eat."

"Good idea." Daniel buckled the leather bag against his chest and pulled his cloak over it.

"I'll send word when I've talked to Horace." He patted Ysabel's shoulder and left the room.

After he passed through the castle gates, Ysabel started for the door, intending to walk back to her village. She wanted to wait for Daniel to return, but Olenna would wake soon and wonder at her absence.

Her snakebite began to itch. Ysabel rubbed it then stopped and looked at the scar. Her heart beat faster as she thrust her hand into her waistbag. She touched the gold coin and pulled it out. She tossed the glowing coin into the air and caught it in her hand. The image of King Jeramin faced upward with his sword pointing toward the North Woods. She put the coin on the table and spun it on its edge. Ysabel scratched her scar as she waited for the coin to stop. It fell with the sword aimed north. She placed the coin on its edge again and smiled, knowing before it stopped spinning that the coin would come to rest with the sword pointing north.

She hummed a tune as she dropped it into her waistbag. She wouldn't return to the cottage right away; the coin had shown that she was to go to the North Woods and find Horace. Olenna wouldn't worry; she would see the coin on the table and believe that Ysabel had gone to the castle to visit Daniel.

Ysabel gazed at the items on Daniel's worktable. Balls of leather string were lined up against the wall. Some of the strings were as delicate as embroidery thread; others were thick cords. She grabbed a ball of fine leather thread and the case of bronze needles and tucked them into her waistbag. She thought Daniel wouldn't mind if she took the needle and thread; Horace's cloak might need mending.

She heard the sound of a horn and looked through the window at a messenger riding through the gates. He held up a pole flying the king's banner; a black boar with flaming red eyes.

The pastry cook and several girls stepped out of the kitchen, wiping their floured hands on their aprons. The master and one of his boys hurried from the stables.

"King Jeramin arrives at midday," the messenger yelled. He dismounted, threw the reins to the stable boy and hastened toward the doors of the great hall. The cook waved her apron at the girls, shooing them back into the kitchen while the boy led the horse to the stables.

Ysabel retied her waistbag and ran from the armory toward the gates. Two guards stood together, talking about the king's injury. A clean wound, said one as he waved her through the gates. He was fortunate, said the other, the tusk went through the side of his belly without catching his guts.

Daniel was a small figure in the distance, walking quickly toward the North Woods. Ysabel raced across the lumpy soil, not slowing until she was close enough to call Daniel's name.

"The king returns at midday," she said when he turned around. "We have to warn Horace."

Daniel shouted the giant's name when they entered the woods. After a moment, something dark dropped from the sky in front of them. Ysabel looked up to see Soleigh swaying on a branch above her head. She heard a deep voice in the woods, Horace calling for the young Anthra. Daniel yelled Horace's name again and the trees around them seemed to bend under the giant's joyful shout of welcome. Soleigh cawed in response and jumped upward from branch to branch until she reached the top of the tree.

She launched herself into the blue sky. Daniel and Ysabel ran headlong through the woods, leaping over fallen branches and crashing through bushes as they followed the Anthra soaring high above them, leading them to their friend.

Note from Signe Kopps

Thank you for reading Anthra's Moon. If you enjoyed it, please take a moment to leave a review on Amazon, Barnes and Noble, or other fine online bookstores.

I welcome contact and comments from readers. You can reach me to leave comments or to join my mailing list on my website: signekopps.com

-- Signe Kopps

69112105R00106

Made in the USA
San Bernardino, CA
12 February 2018